Carlos

A catalog record for this book is available from the Library of Congress

ISBN: 0692057498
ISBN 13: 9780692057490

From error to error one discovers the entire truth.

—Sigmund Freud

ONE

It is early in the morning—4:00 a.m., to be precise. I am going into work early so that I can train before I have to deal with the bullshit of other people. It is my time of solace. Except there is no solace. There should be, but there isn't.

The gym doesn't open until 5:00 a.m., so for all intents and purposes, I should be alone. Today I am training with Bennie, if he can manage to get up, which is his usual bullshit. I have decided that I don't care if he makes it or not. I just won't go as heavy. I can use the alone time, anyway.

Bennie is waiting for me when I pull into the parking lot, sipping at a coffee and staring at his phone, probably porn. My oldest friend is a porn junkie, so it would sort of be a major surprise if he *wasn't* watching it. Since he doesn't look up as I pull in, I assume today isn't the day I get the shock of my twenty-nine-year life.

I lock my car and make my way to Bennie. He still doesn't grace me with as much as a glance from his phone.

"Seriously, Ben?"

"It's not what you think," he says.

"It isn't?"

"No. I'm not into porn anymore."

"I find that very difficult to believe, Ben."

Thing is, he still doesn't look up. Finally, I make my way around to get a peek at what he can't take his eyes off. Much to my surprise, Bennie has been telling me the truth; he isn't watching porn. What he is watching is a young woman sleeping. Granted, she is in a red tank top and matching boy shorts, and her body looks ridiculous, yet she isn't doing anything but sleeping.

I look at my friend, who still doesn't look at me. He is deep into whatever the fuck he is into. "What?" he asks finally.

"Nothing, Ben. Are you coming inside to train? I have a time limit."

"Yeah, Shep, I'm down," he says, finally taking his eyes off the phone.

We walk in silence for a few steps as we get to the locked door of Insane! Fitness. I want to inquire as to what my buddy's fetish de jour is, but I decide against it. We don't hang out like we used to, and to spend time on such a subject feels like a waste.

I settle on, "How's Amy?"

"Ugh."

"That good?"

"She wants to start a family, Shep. I half expect her to poke holes in the condoms at this point."

"Jesus, that baby crazy?"

"Yep, that's the operating theory. She won't even fuck me before we have 'the talk.'"

"Yikes."

I unlock the door, and Bennie and I move inside. There are lights on that shouldn't be on.

"They forget to kill them every night," I say to Bennie, pointing skyward.

"Who gives a shit? Can't corporate globo gym cover a few extra bucks for lighting?"

"You would think—these fuckers love to cut corners."

Bennie walks ahead of me, climbing the stairs. He stops suddenly. "You hear that?"

I move next to him. There is a sound, more like a dull moan. "What the fuck is that?"

We both look up the stairs, and as we do, the moaning grows louder.

"Sounds like people fucking," Bennie says with a slick smile.

"That does sound like fucking."

"Let's check it out."

I shrug my shoulders. What I want is my solace; then, again, I'd also like to know who is fucking in the gym at this hour, or any hour for that matter. There aren't so many people with keys besides the manager, the janitors, and some trainers.

We stop outside the men's locker room. It is clear that this is where the noise is coming from.

"It sounds like two dudes," Bennie not-so-astutely deduces.

"It *is* a men's room, Ben."

"I gotta know."

"Seriously? Come on, man; leave whoever it is alone. I only have so much time to train."

Bennie looks severely disappointed. "Fuck it; let's lift." He starts to walk but then stops. "You really don't want to know what dudes are boning each other?"

"I'm all set on that, but go nuts or join in with them; sorta seems like you want to."

"Fuck you, Shep."

TWO

The majority of the weight-training equipment is on the third floor, cardio and ab mats on the second with the lockers, and pool and reception on the first. The place is massive. It is the epitome of a corporate gym. I wish it were a better place to work, at least from a financial standpoint. I am a personal trainer, which is really a misnomer. I am mostly a shrink, a sounding board, and, on occasion, a guy who helps people progress physically. I see a revolving door of personas, only a handful of whom are tolerable. It's a job. What can I tell you?

It started one summer during college. I had always trained anyway, and three sports in high school inadvertently prepared me for an adult life I hadn't planned on. I had never envisioned making a lifelong career out of it; I just meant to make a few bucks, training a few people, but that snowballed into year after year after year of working at the same place, doing the same thing, adding more clients. I somehow joined the grind. At first I worked under the table, uncertified, wholly unofficial with family, friends, and whatnot. But then I went for my certification and was offered employment as an official trainer at Insane! Fitness.

When Bennie and I come downstairs, we dare to go into the locker room. I am relieved to find it empty, although I am not sure I can say the same for my boy. He seems to scan the area with his eyes and ears with a certain disappointment.

"Damn," Ben says.

I chuckle a bit. Bennie has always been a bit strange, and although I am used to it, I cannot say that I can wrap my head around his mind. Ben is a creative; he is starting to make a living as a metal sculptor. Apparently, he is good at it, as people pay him to make odd bits of art to put inside and outside their homes. On occasion, I make a few bucks helping him install whatever it is he has been commissioned for. He stands about six feet and is lean and muscular. The boy is vain; then again, no one could fault him. Bennie meets and seduces more women than anyone I know. He has a long-term girlfriend, but that doesn't stop him from being on a constant prowl. Plus, I'm pretty sure that he believes he has a constant hall pass. He doesn't. Granted, he is a good-looking guy, but there must be something else. He isn't *that* good looking.

"I gotta drop a deuce."

"And you are telling me this why?" I ask.

"Male bonding?" he says, shrugging, headed to the toilets.

I go downstairs. It is still early, but I see Rack sitting at his computer. Jason "Rack" Rackowski is Insane! Fitness's general manager. He hears me coming down the stairs and turns suddenly.

"Jesus, Shep, don't fucking sneak up on me like that!"

I stop and look at him wondering what he is talking about. I think the dude has injected several steroids too many. He goes back to what he seems to be doing perpetually, staring at his computer. I take that as a sign that I can safely keep it moving. I hop over the counter to the smoothie bar and make myself some protein. I have about ten minutes before my first client. I try to relish the solace. Bennie comes down.

"You want one?" I ask, lifting my sixty grams of protein.

"Nah, I need some real food. What's with him?" Ben asks, gesturing to Rack.

"I dunno. Too many drugs is my guess."

"So I saw a guy in the men's cleaning—must be a janitor. Spanishy. You think him and Rack were bumping the nasty?"

I practically spit my shake all over the counter of the smoothie bar. "No, man, Rack has a superhot girlfriend."

"What the hell does that matter? Maybe he is an equal-opportunity fornicator."

"Sure, man, that must be it. Same time tomorrow? Maybe some back work?"

"Sounds good."

We fist-bump, and my buddy leaves. The janitor he was talking about comes down the stairs; he exchanges a look with Rack before noticing me. The exchange seems to have been truncated.

THREE

Brie makes me want to commit hara-kiri; an honorable death is the best I can hope for. The woman is simply incorrigible. Most clients train with a pro because they lack both motivation and knowledge base. Brie doesn't lack the motivation; she likes to work out, but, sadly, she has spent a lifetime training incorrectly. This makes her question my highly certified and correct instruction. It is beyond insufferable, other than the fact that she has paid Insane! Fitness two years in advance for training sessions three times per week.

I wish she wouldn't have for multiple reasons. The sales guys sign up people for training, and they get a commission; plus, the gym gets their cut. I end up with the smallest piece of the pie, roughly ten dollars per half hour. It's actually a twenty-five-minute session, but I don't nickel-and-dime my clients. Twenty dollars an hour (before taxes, mind you) isn't horrible, but it isn't so great either. Some of the people I train aren't worth the money for the level of annoyance they provide. Other clients are great, but those are fewer and further in between. In a perfect world, I would have a majority of clients pay me cash under the table. Brie, as insufferable as she is, probably could be talked into such a mutually beneficial arrangement, but she thought the sales guy was flirting with her, and so she did whatever she needed to do to perpetuate the flirtation. I guess I can't blame her; she looks good for her age. She is pushing sixty. A steroid-assisted salesman, probably less than half her age, paying attention to her is cougar catnip. Besides her age, she is slender, with monster boobs and skinny toothpick legs. All my buddies who come in while I am training her tell me they would fuck her, and I do not doubt it. Brie is attractive; she would be more so if she would actually listen instead of bucking me at every turn.

"Am I doing this right, Shep?"

I admit that sometimes I check out when I train. It is wholly unprofessional, but it happens as if it is some sort of defense mechanism designed not to make me lose my shit on these people.

"Well, Brie, no, you are not. Do you need me to show you again?"

"Is it better like this?"

"Um...no, Brie, it isn't. I think I should maybe demonstrate so you can get the right idea."

"What about this way?"

I pause, knowing that if I perpetuate this, it will never end. "Looking good, Brie, looking good."

I resume checking out status. I believe I have mastered the look that appears as if I am interested, while not paying an iota of attention at all. It is my saving grace. I am so, so damn good at it, I probably could teach a separate certification in that alone. Lord knows the other trainers could use the skill set.

FOUR

There are currently three other trainers on staff at Insane! Fitness. One is a woman named Lucy, who is in her early thirties and scores all the old men and housewives. She's nice and respectful, although I can't say we interact all that much. Lucy has a long-term boyfriend and seems to shy away from the men who try and flirt and pick her up.

The other two are men of varying ages. Michael is older, maybe in his fifties or sixties. He hasn't too many clients; often, he gets stuck with the bottom-of-the-barrel types who aren't going to stick with any program. Michael is a dinosaur, as are most of his clients. The one thing he is, though, is loyal. Most people cut their teeth at Insane! Fitness and then sail off to greener pastures; for Michael, *this* is the pasture.

Ezra is my main competition to get clients. He is twenty-five and shredded. He may look better than me with his shirt off, or on for that matter, but I attribute that to his color, and by color I mean his blackness. He has been at Insane! for a year, which is about the only category I beat him on, as I've worked at the gym for just over four years. One could say Ezra is the new me, just darker. The difference being, hue aside, that clients request him. Although the hue differential may be what is tipping the scales in his favor. I don't know why, but for some reason, black muscular guys are more attractive to, say, everyone. I would cry racism, but you know.

We all meet once a week with Rack, unless we can think of ways to slink out of these useless meetings. They are pretty much always the same: up our sales numbers with clients in terms of sessions, generate new clients, no under-the-table, training, dress, and appearance codes. Most of these I do not follow, nor do many of my coworkers. I honestly don't know why we have these meetings at all.

Four of us are there, everyone except Ezra; now that I think about it, I wonder if he ever has made a meeting. I know he is at the gym somewhere.

"So, guys, we need to get the sales numbers up," Rack says, talking about a hundred miles an hour. "Let your clients know the company will make long-term deals; the longer the commit, the cheaper the sessions."

"Yeah, and the less money for us, right, Rack?" Michael barks.

Lucy and I share a look and laugh.

"You have the least amount of clients, Mike. You are lucky to be making *any* money."

"I don't need this shit, Rack. I'm outta here." Michael stands and walks off.

"He's right. We do the same crap every week, man. How about we do it once a month? Or less," I say.

"I vote for less," Lucy adds.

"Less it is then," I agree.

Rack puts his hands on his hips and stares. It is one of those viciously uncomfortable looks that you really don't know what is going to happen next, but you realize that the odds of it being good are relatively nonexistent.

Lucy looks at Rack and then at me; when nothing happens, she gets up to leave. That's when steam may have well begun shooting of out

Rack's ears. He slams his palm down on his desk, making everything on top of it, desktop and all, leap up about an inch before crashing back down in a tumult of disarray.

"Sit the fuck down."

"You are tripping out, Rack. You can't talk to me—or us—like this. You need to ease up on that shit," Lucy tells him.

I put my hands up in an offer of peace. Rack looks like he is an aneurysm waiting to happen. It's not so much of a secret that he juices, but that may not be all that is on the menu. I've heard rumors that he likes to party and that guys I know from the gym have seen him snort white powder in men's rooms at local bars, but who knows. What I am sure of is that he seems tightly wound.

Lucy leaves. Rack flits his eyes toward her but stays focused on me, so I stay seated.

"Shep, you are the only one who stayed," he says, exasperated.

"It's just a gym, Rack," I say finally when it seems clear he's got nothing else.

I look him in the eyes and slap his back as I move past him. I don't look back, and he doesn't call after me.

FIVE

I leave the gym for the first time in hours. I generally have a morning crush and then a lull, where, if I am lucky, I can get a nap and recharge before I start the afternoon and evening sessions.

Fortunately, I live about a ten-minute drive away from Insane! Fitness. Elmwood, Connecticut, is a small town about fifty minutes outside New York City. I grew up here, went to school here, and I guess I can't get my sorry ass out. Maybe it is one of those rhythm-of-life scenarios, where one is stuck in a perpetual loop of shitty circles.

I wish I were surprised. I have seen the same thing happen to other members of my family. My father is still around despite the fact he is retired and divorced from my mother. My mother is still here too, despite the fact she lost her job a while back and is divorced from my father. My sisters both have families and live locally as well. We just can't fucking get out of Elmwood; such is the Shepard curse.

I get home, and my divorced parents are sitting in the kitchen, coexisting somehow in some sort of terrible silence. It is that homemade awkwardness that you just can't manufacture.

My mom is short and in shape. She started training with me and various in-shape girlfriends over the years, after she and my father called it quits. You would think that my dad would have done the same, and he does work out, on occasion, but not how you would think a divorced man, with what one would think of as a few miles left in the tank, might push it. Dad has seemingly given up, or maybe, just maybe, he thinks he still has a shot with mom. He definitely does not.

"Hi, Luke, I made some chicken salad, if you are hungry."

"Thanks, Ma."

My dad just looks at me and rolls his eyes. He has his arms crossed in a defensive posture. I wonder if they have been arguing. I opt for the nap that I desperately need instead of eating.

My dad has not handled the divorce well. I am not sure who does handle divorce in a positive manner, but whatever he has done, it isn't that. It seems clear that he has given up. It is disturbing. I wish things were different. I wish my parents weren't split at all, but they live with me now, in a bizarre broken family dynamic, despite it being clear we are not the unified front we once were.

Aria is naked in bed, passed out. I stop and admire her beauty. She sleeps with her forearm draped over her eyes, one perky breast exposed. Aria and I have been official for about three months. She is twenty-five, stands about five foot two, and is lucky if she weighs one hundred pounds. I move to the bed and stroke her long dark hair. I don't want to wake her, as I know she has been bartending all night and actually came in after I left to meet Bennie at 4:00 a.m.

"Hey," she says, opening her eyes gently.

"Sorry, I didn't mean to get you up."

"You gunna fuck me or what?"

"I need to take a shower."

"OK, what are you waiting for?"

I decide that I do not know what I am waiting for. A beautiful woman has asked me to fuck her. I have a quick shower. Aria comes in wearing one of my tank tops as I am getting out of the shower. I ogle her side boob and her toned legs, and she notices my erection in the mirror while she brushes her teeth. She smiles as I drop my towel and make may way to her, best as a man can in my condition.

Aria keeps brushing her teeth as I put myself inside her, never taking her eyes off me as I pound away. Finally, she drops the toothbrush in the sink as she climaxes. The sight and sound of her getting off gets me off too, and I collapse on her. Aria takes the opportunity to rinse out her mouth from the toothpaste residue.

"You could be a dentist, if you promoted that brushing regimen," she tells me.

"Who said I'm not?"

"Good point. My turn to get clean."

"Meet me back in bed?"

Aria nods and gives me a seductive smile before hopping in the shower.

My bed seems like an oasis. It just feels good to lay there in a postcoital nothingness. I can probably nap for a couple of hours, but my bet is on a second session with Aria and us catching up. We have been like two ships passing in the night lately, and it has us both a bit frustrated.

That is my life to date. It's pretty sad, pushing thirty, and none of it is how I envisioned. Aria is great, but I have misgivings as to whether it will last. It's not her; it's me. I do this; I am a serial monogamist. If three to nine months of one woman at a time qualifies. Aria is different, or should I say, she is the latest different. She works hard at a bar/restaurant, making money flirting with customers as she makes them drinks. It's all part of the job, and I'm OK with it. Aria knows she is a beautiful woman; why not use her talents to her advantage? It isn't like women, and some men, don't flirt with me at work. Fortunately, we don't do jealous. I have had bad psychotic experiences with jealous women, and it is not any fun at all. The irony is that the jealous ones always have reasons to suspect, because they are cheaters. What a joke, but 100 percent of the time that's the deal.

I lie in bed and stare at the ceiling. Part of me is waiting for Aria to come back for round two; part of me hope she goes home so I can sleep. This is a rare moment of solitude for me. I both love it and hate it. I've heard from more than one source that I don't like being alone. It may be true; I rarely am and have limited opportunity to test the theory. Between the serial monogamy, the job and my family, about the only time I have to myself is when I take a shit, sometimes not even then. I shit a lot at the gym.

"What are you thinkin' about?" Aria asks, standing in the doorway, wearing nothing but a towel.

Aria has the body of a fitness model. My cock gets hard fast.

"Nothing important."

Aria closes the door, drops her towel, and comes to bed. Round two has begun. *Fuck alone.*

SIX

I lumber back to work at 4:30 p.m. Mercifully, my first client canceled, and I actually *did* get a brief catnap in. I don't know how long I can keep this pace. I recharge a bit over the weekend, but not altogether so much because I still have a family, a girlfriend, and friends who all seem to need and want attention of some sort. It's a vicious circle.

<u>where are you?????</u>

I look at my phone. It's Jenna, my client, whom I am exactly one minute late for, as I am walking in the door of Insane! Fitness. I let out a long sigh. I made the mistake of sleeping with Jenna before Aria and after Charlize.

I don't bother returning the text; instead, I ignore the staff and people I know, all of whom try to engage me as I bound up to the training station on the third floor. Jenna is standing there, arms crossed. She has a nice body, although I attribute that to good genes rather than work I have done with her or that she has done on her own. Jenna has a pretty face, sort of round and chubby, mostly because she is a class A boozehound. I see her out locally on the rare occasions I imbibe. Truth be told, this is how we hooked up the handful of times we did. Totally unprofessional, I realize this, and potentially very, very stupid of me. I could have been fired if anyone of consequence found out.

Jenna is short but not really petite, not really thick. She clearly is annoyed at my ninety seconds of lateness. Her arms remain crossed as I approach.

"I thought you were blowing me off."

She says this despite the fact I have never missed a session with her, or anyone else for that matter, without ample and reasonable notification.

"Why would you think that?"

"Shit, Shep, you're late, and you didn't return my text!" Jenna says in total seriousness.

On a lesser day, I may not be as focused as to not flip out on her. I deal with a myriad of personas, most of whom are of the asshole variety. I take a deep breath.

"I had an issue getting a spot. I circled for"

"I expect you to make up for the lost time, Shep," she says, cutting me off.

"Uh...yeah, sure thing."

"Not today, though; I don't have a second to spare."

Ninety seconds. "Well, then, we better get started."

It takes me all of two or three seconds into the session to check out. I train Jenna on autopilot, thankfully. I register that we are talking, but I cannot attest to what is said.

"Shep!"

I snap out of it and look at her.

"You gunna answer me?"

"Uh…"

"Are you working late?"

"Oh, yeah, sorry, I had to think about the schedule. Yes, Jenna, I am."

"Well, if you feel like meeting me out later, and I dunno, maybe we can hang out?"

"Oh wow, yeah, I really want to. Can I text you later when I get done?"

"Sure," she says, smiling at me as she floats away.

It's unbelievable; she treats me like the help and then wants to "hang out," which means fuck. What a mistake it was hooking up with her, or maybe women are just insane, and men are equally insane.

Brandon comes late to the session. He comes late to every session, as if someone had suggested he work with a trainer, but he really doesn't want to. Since I generally go from one client to the next, if they come fifteen minutes late, there isn't much I can do. Not that I want to do anything, mind you. I need to get paid, and unless they cancel with twenty-four hours' notice, I do get money for the session whether they come on time or at all.

"Sorry, Shep, I got caught up at work."

"No skin off my back, Brandon, but we have ten minutes left. I have a client scheduled after you."

"It's my fault; maybe we can talk nutrition. I'm not feeling it today."

Brandon hasn't felt it at all, not today, not ever. He does come in to the gym on his own, which is more than I can say for, say, 70 percent of my clientele, but aside from dropping a lot of weight from the get-go, he has plateaued. I didn't know him when he was tipping the scales at three hundred pounds plus; he came to me after a pizza and ice-cream heavy detox.

"Sure," I say, grateful for something different.

"Can we go to the smoothie bar? I could use something."

"Why not?"

Brandon and I go down to the first floor. I ogle so many women on the way down that my eyeballs hurt. Many of them ogle me right back, even though most know I have a girlfriend; they also know that I may have a new one in a few months and that it could be them.

"Wow, you know so many women."

"I have worked here for years...comes with the territory."

"Could you introduce me to some?"

"Sure," I say, knowing in my heart of hearts that it won't matter.

Once downstairs, I expect Brandon to have a high-protein shake, because we have discussed upping his protein. Instead, he opts for a bar— granted, it's a protein bar, but one that is loaded with sugar alcohol and is not the snack of choice for someone still trying to drop pounds.

"Do you like this brand?" he asks me as he simultaneously destroys the bar.

"It's got some junk in it, Brandon."

"I thought it was a protein bar."

"It is; they just aren't all built the same. If it has sugar alcohol in it, that can be deceptive; it's used to keep the actual sugar numbers down, but, truthfully, you are better off with sugar. It gets a bad rap."

"Oh," he says with certain dejection, wiping a gob of chocolate–peanut butter mix off his lips.

"Next time. The main thing is getting into healthy habits. What did you have today?"

"For breakfast I had a bagel with peanut butter. Lunch, I had a pastrami and corned beef on rye, with russian dressing, and then I had a bag of M&Ms."

"So I think you would see some results with less sugar and more protein, healthy carbs."

"What's a good carb?"

"Sweet potatoes."

"I like those."

"Me too."

"Hi, Shep," Charlize says, waving at me, a hint of seduction in her eyes.

"Hey."

"Wow, who was that?"

"That was Charlize, my ex."

"Is it in bad taste for me to ask you to hook me up with her?"

"Yeah, Brandon, it is." I pause. "Chicken breast or other lean proteins, steamed veggies, nothing white: rice, potato, or pasta. Start there, plan your meals, no fast food, and if you can prep for the day in advance, even better. The other thing you can do is keep a food journal; people do that and have success in watching the intake, but, Brandon, coming in and weight training will really help you drop pounds."

"I will, Shep; I know I've been slacking."

"No worries, man. I gotta run; my next client is here."

SEVEN

Friday night has arrived, finally. I work Monday through Thursday until at least 9:00 p.m. I am stuck between needing to unwind by going out or needing to relax by staying in.

Aria is working, but she works at a bar and wants me to come hang out. I can kill several birds with one stone, since Bennie wants to go out with another buddy, Max. Being that we live in Connecticut, the nightlife is a bit limited. It's dinner, drinks, and more drinks, until about 2:00 a.m. Or it's a house party, and being that it is summer, I know of a few.

There is no one home when I get back. This fact thrills me to no end. I have a rare moment of being alone. The first thing I do is roll a joint. I grab a beer from the fridge and go out to my deck, and my dog, Arther the beagle, pads out behind me. I smoke half the jay and then relax in the bliss of being ridiculously baked on a temperate day with just a beer and a beagle. It is bliss.

In my blissful haze, I contemplate life. Mine isn't what I had hoped for. I fell into the pro-trainer thing mostly because I had initially failed at public service. I took tests for fire, police, and EMT jobs. I made it through various rounds of interviews and testing for all three, but an offer never materialized. In theory, I could still test for these jobs, but it has less appeal for me at almost thirty than it did at twenty-two. I would have been eight years into a juicy pension, and I cannot get those days back. Truth is, aside from the decent notion of helping the community, it was a steady job, with insurance.

The bonus of my life, as it turned out, is that I am not tethered to any one location. I have often thought about leaving Elmwood. I could transfer to any Insane! Fitness gym; there are hundreds of locations around the country. I contemplate California. SoCal. People take the fitness lifestyle seriously, which makes them a joy to work with, as opposed to people who are convinced that training with a pro for twenty-five minutes a week will seriously change the way they look or feel.

It is nice, the solace. I feel for a few moments, at least, as if the weight of life is off my back, although I know I will have to reload the weight back on soon enough. I guess it isn't so horrible; I have a home that I have equity in, although I have twenty-five years' worth of payments left before I own it outright. I could rent it, pay it down, and make a couple of bucks in the meantime. That would mean my parents would have to leave and find a place, but I have siblings. *Why didn't they take them, anyway?* There is food on the table and a woman with whom to share a bed. The world has all these horrors; what right do I have to complain? I don't. Yet I am not content. I am lost. I have taken the path that life has given me, rather than fight for what I truly wanted. *I hate myself.*

Inside I hear my phone dinging with a litany of texts, e-mails, FB posts, and Snapchats. I should have turned the ringer off. Here we go again; I am the victim, despite the fact I am actually popular. *What an asshole.*

I finish my beer and lumber inside. I look at my phone and respond to Ben and Max. Then I turn off the phone and hit the bed; smoking always makes me drowsy.

EIGHT

Bennie and Max pick me up despite the fact I am the least likely to drink myself stupid. Max is driving, and Bennie is sitting in the passenger seat with his eyes glued to his phone. I slip in the back seat. Max hands me a beer.

"Thanks, dude."

"Where we going?" Max asks.

I have been friends with Max for my entire life. Much like me, he has eaten the shit life has served up. His takes the form of working at his stepfather's hardware store. I haven't seen him for a while other than when he pops in to feign a workout. It is always at night when the visuals are at their peak. Max rarely has a girlfriend, but, boy, does he love the casual thing. He is a decent-looking guy, but what he may lack in looks, he makes up with persona. Everyone likes him; he knows how to work a room, a crowd, especially women but also men.

"Let's go see Aria first."

Bennie makes the whip sound, without looking up from his phone. I peek, and he is watching another beautiful young woman sleeping in some seductive outfit.

"Look, I don't give a shit where we go. It's a deep discount on drinks, which I figured you cheap fucks would be on board with."

"Chill out, Shep," Max says. "It's cool we go to Aria's."

"OK, then," I say, melting into the back seat.

Aria works at a Spanish restaurant that doubles as a bar once food is out of the way. She works a lot, Wednesday to Saturday prime hours.

She knows the owner; he is friends with someone in her family. It's nice that there is a concept of community within different racial and religious groups, although white people do not seem to be on that page. It isn't like the owner is doing her a huge favor; Aria is stunning and affable, not to mention a good bartender. She is fast and flirty; everyone keeps coming back for more.

We get there, and it is in mid-segue between the dinner and the bar hoppers. It's the weekend, so the kitchen is open until midnight. We saddle up at the bar. Aria is slammed between both crowds slaking the pressures of the week away. Max and Bennie scan the crowd around the bar; fuckers are always on the hunt. I sit and try to wait patiently as Aria mixes drinks and pays attention to what seems to be everyone but me. I am not the jealous type, but I admit that sometimes it bothers me. Finally, she sees me, and her face brightens considerably, which makes me feel better.

"Hey! You hungry or just thirsty?" she asks, touching my arm.

"Both."

"What about your girlfriends?"

"Nice seeing you too, Aria," Max says.

"Don't get bitchy with me, Maxine."

Bennie laughs but doesn't remove his eyes from his phone. It is unclear what he finds so funny.

"What are you laughing at? More porn?" Aria asks Bennie.

Bennie looks up at her. "No. I'm off that shit."

"Yeah, he's on some entirely different thing now," Max tells her.

"I don't want to know," Aria says. "Tequila? Food?"

I ask for the special burrito and a beer. Max and Bennie are on all-liquid diets. Aria looks at me and smiles. There is a gleam in her eye, and for a brief moment, we are the only people there despite being in a crowded room. And then she is off bustling making more drinks, taking more orders, talking to staff and customers with a dervish-like energy.

I turn toward the restaurant side, joining my comrades as they stare out at the people. Bennie seems to steal glances over his obsessive phone bullshit. Max elbows my arm several times as attractive women in groups enter the place or sidle up to the bar. I look, of course, but I am a loyal guy, and that is about all I will do.

At one point I turn, and I see Aria at the far end of the bar. She is speaking with one of the staff...a waiter? Then it happens...an exchange so smooth that everyone could have easily missed it despite looking directly at it. It looks like a drug deal. I have not known Aria to use drugs, aside from a few drinks and maybe a hit off a joint. *This is something else.*

Max smacks me out of my shock. "Dude, doesn't that blonde go to Insane?"

I look, still stymied by what I have seen, or thought I have seen. I don't tell Aria what she can and cannot do, nor do I want to, but I also am not into having a girlfriend doing heavy shit. "Yeah, that's Gwen. I thought you hung out with her last year."

"Uh...no, I would have remembered a dime like that."

"She wasn't a dime last year; she was a six, all on account of the eighty-pound difference."

"Really?"

"That was your rating, not mine, but she does look great." I pause. "I am going to talk to Aria."

Max nods, without removing his stare from Gwen. I shake my head and turn to see if I can grab Aria's attention, but she is gone. I ask the bar back where she went, and he points me to the ladies'.

I am standing outside the bathroom when she comes out.

"Hey," she says seductively.

"Look, I don't want to ask, but I have to. I saw you at the end of the bar. You wanna tell me what that was?"

I am hoping that there is a reasonable explanation for what I thought I saw; instead, what comes is a head bow.

"Not really," she says finally. "I gotta get back."

"But you had time for whatever—"

"I'm sorry, Shep; can we talk about this later?"

"I don't see the point, Aria."

Back at the bar, my burrito has arrived. I have lost my appetite. Max is talking to Gwen and pawing at her at the same time. Bennie is staring at his phone. I sit back down despite the fact I want to leave, and badly. Thankfully Gwen leaves for a moment.

"Dude, I am so gunna tap that," Max says.

"That's great, man. Look, I think I'm gunna Uber home."

"What? Why?"

"It's a long story, but I see you are doing well here, and I have no fucking clue what Bennie is doing, but I gotta go."

Max knows me well enough to know when I am about to pop. He nods. "I will take you."

"I'm good, man."

I put twenty dollars under the plate of uneaten burrito. I look at Aria; she is making drinks and doesn't even look my way.

NINE

I take an Ambien when I get home and down it with a beer. I know I won't sleep without it, and I have no desire to have my head fucking with me all night. It still takes me a long time to pass out when it shouldn't; between the workweek and the sleep aid and booze, I should be comatose...

I wake up groggy as hell. I want to stay in bed all day long. I am not surprised that I wake up alone. I assume at some point Aria and I will talk, but she made the wise move and stayed away.

I lumber out of bed and into the bathroom. I take my time. There seems to be peace and quiet, and I drink it in like a thirsty man who has just crawled through the desert.

After, I make my way downstairs. My mom is making eggs and bacon. My dad sits in that awkward silence he seems to live in perpetually. I join him in the silence and wonder if that is the secret sauce to keeping people who are close to each other sane.

"Aria didn't come home last night?" my mother asks, handing me a plate of food.

"She doesn't live here, Mom."

My father shoots me a look.

"I like her, Luke. She is responsible, and respectful," my mother injects.

My eyes don't deviate from my eggs. All I can think is how irresponsible and disrespectful drugs are to a relationship.

"It would be nice if you could settle on one girl, maybe think about giving us some grandchildren," Mom says.

"Sure, Mom. My priority is keeping you in kids to take care of."

I finish quickly and take my plate to the sink. My mother intercepts me and takes the flatware.

"I'm just saying it would be nice for us if you were settled."

"I know."

I go back to my room to isolate. *It would be nice to be settled. Whatever that really means.*

TEN

We need to talk

I get a text from Aria when I am at the gym training alone. I don't answer. I don't want to. I am taking out all my frustrations on the weights. I don't want my relationship to be over, but I am not OK with what I saw.

I stay at Insane! Fitness for two hours lifting and then another hour talking bullshit with some of the regulars. I am in full avoidance mode.

**I know you are angry. Pls give me a chance to explain.**

I sigh at the text. I really don't care. That's a lie. I _do_ care. I wish I didn't.

**Meet me at the coffee place.**

**K Half hr?**

Yeah

I am twenty minutes late. It wasn't on purpose. Well, it wasn't consciously on purpose. Aria is sitting wringing her hands nervously.

"Hey," she says.

I sit wordlessly, somehow invoking the silent DNA of my father.

"You won't talk to me?" she asks.

"I'm here, Aria."

"Shep, last night, it wasn't what you think."

"Well, what I think was you were doing drugs. Hard ones."

"Yeah, that's right; I did buy some."

"So, it _is_ what I thought."

"I didn't do them."

"That's nice, Aria. Look, I'm not going to tell you what you can or can't do, but I don't want to be with someone who chooses that lifestyle. So, if we are done here, I'm going home. I will put whatever stuff together that you left at the house, and you can come get it when I am not there, OK?"

I get up, resolved that I am doing what is best despite the fact I feel for Aria. I am walking away when she calls my name. I know I shouldn't turn, but there is something in her voice that causes me go against the grain on what I know. When I turn back to her, she has a vulnerable look so delicate that she looks as if she may shatter.

"I'm pregnant."

I feel myself buckle. I make my way back to Aria.

"I just found out this morning. I can pee on another stick if you don't believe me."

I look at her wondering why she would say that.

"Say something, Shep."

"I thought you were on the pill."

"I am."

"What happened then?"

"It isn't one hundred percent is what happened."

I nod. This is the third girlfriend I have gotten pregnant. I should know better.

"What do you want to do?" she asks me.

"What do you?" I deflect expertly.

"I would like to start a family."

This revelation, coming in Starbucks of all places. "What happened last night?"

"Shep..."

"I think you need to tell me."

"I've been pushing at work. It just keeps me alert."

"Coke?"

"Yeah."

"Classic mom stuff."

"Fuck you, Shep," she says, getting up suddenly and storming off.

I sit there, dumbfounded by so many things that it is hard to pinpoint which has me ground down worse.

ELEVEN

I go home and shower, followed by lying down and praying for death. When death doesn't come, I contemplate my options. I laugh at the silliness of life; we are peppered with choices, but how many are our own? When I think of it, I realize that my life is a culmination of being superfucked and cornered into most situations. I do not want to raise a kid under such auspices. I am not sure I want to have a family at all, since I am already not so thrilled with the one I already have. Add to this that I have been seeing Aria for only about ninety days and that we didn't plan this, and it feels like a disaster. And then there are the drugs; how long had that been going on?

Thoughts pepper my head so fast and hard that it feels like my brain may break.

WTF was that about last nite??

Max is texting me. I ignore him. I turn off my phone. I roll a joint and go downstairs, hoping neither parent is lurking. I move out to my deck and light up. I usually don't smoke so much, but if I don't do anything to slow myself down, I may never relax.

"Luke!"

I turn to see my mom. It is an awkward moment. I should feel caught, but this is my house, so I really don't care if my mother has an issue with me getting lifted. She can move out and take her ex-husband with her.

"Yeah, Ma?"

"Is that weed?"

"Yep."

"Can I smoke with you?"

I look at my mother with a newfound adoration. "Sure."

She comes out, and we pass the joint back and forth as if this is a regular deal between us. It isn't. I had no idea my mom liked pot. It is a nice few moments of silence. I get along with my mother; I would venture to say we are friends. Smoking some weed together, I am pretty sure, cements the bond.

"What's going on with you?" she asks.

"Shit, I wish I knew. Early onset midlife crisis?"

"I assumed Aria."

"Yeah, she's in the mix."

"You do tend to get like this with women."

"Ugh, I know. I haven't a clue what I am doing."

"It's OK, Luke; no one really does. Look at me and your father. All these years, and not together, but still here. Try figuring that out."

"You think I don't?"

We laugh uncontrollably for a while, hug it out, and then I go back to the isolation of my room. Alone again.

It's funny because on the one hand I like the solitude, but on the flip side, I cannot stand it. I despise Aria for what she has done, but somehow within that, I despise myself too.

I turn my phone back on. I long to hear from Aria but am grateful that she hasn't reached out. What am I supposed to do? There is a text from Max, asking if I want to meet him out for Chinese food. I hit him back and tell him I can be at our go-to joint in twenty minutes.

TWELVE

Max is like Bennie, a lifelong friend. We have seen a lot of each other's ugliness over the years and are still hanging around together. It's a nice bond; we can go swaths of time without seeing each other, yet we know we are there.

"So, Gwen is a blow-job enthusiast," Max tells me.

"That's nice." I chuckle.

We sit and have a beer while we wait for dim sum. I tell him the Aria debacle after he prattles on about the nuances of Gwen's expert blow-jobbing. It is a welcomed distraction.

"So, what are you going to do?"

"Truth is, Max, this is her choice. I'm not going to tell her what she can or can't do with her own body."

"You really think you are getting off that easily? Fuck, when I got Jungle Jane preggers, it was a full-on hormonal dumpster fire. She will want to know what you want; it's like the irrational mama bear syndrome kicks in or something."

"Be that as it may, there are too many issues. It's not like we were trying; she was on birth control."

"Allegedly," Max chimes in.

"Jesus, you think?"

"Women and their need to birth man, even if it wasn't a conscious thing."

"Dude, haven't you impregnated half this town?"

"Yeah, my point exactly."

"Uh. Condom?"

"Really, you are going there right now?"

I swill my beer, grateful that the dim sum has arrived. Max doesn't give it up, though.

"What will you do, Shep?"

"What can I do? Truth is, we didn't want this, and we aren't ready for it either. For Christ's sake, she was doing blow last night. Hopefully things will run their course, and she will make a practical choice."

"A hormonal pregnant woman making a rational choice...tough ask, my friend, tough ask."

"What's up with Bennie?"

"What do you mean?"

"The staring at the sleeping chicks?"

"Oh, yeah, that. It's called vleeping."

"There's a name for it?"

"Yep. It's the latest social-media thing, hot babes sleeping in boy shorts or something sexy.

Well, there are guys too…that would be more for you."

"At this point in time, I wish I were gay—my problems would be different."

"I hear ya." Max then asks, "Those chicks keep looking over here…you know them?"

I look, and I do know them. I don't know why Max asks, because I know the whole town, between living here my whole life and working at a massive gym. They look; I wave.

"The blond one is Sarah something, and the other girl is her friend. Dunno her name."

"We should go over," Max says.

"Can't we just say hello on the way out?"

We pay our bill. There have been lots of waves and smiles. Max and I saunter over, and I introduce my friend. Sarah introduces her cousin, Britt.

"Yeah, I see you guys working out all the time."

"I work out a lot myself; we should train sometime," Max says.

I give him a look.

"Yeah, that would be great!" Cousin Britt says, handing Max her iPhone. "Give me your number."

Max doesn't wait long, expertly pumping his digits in her mobile. When he is done, he puts her phone down, and she pulls up a sleeping chick.

"Oh, vleep a lot?" Max asks.

"I like this one chick, so sexy," Britt answers.

"No guys?"

"Sometimes, but, well, you know."

"I'd like to."

"Yeah, so we gotta bounce; we are...um...meeting friends out," I say, aching to leave.

Now it's Max giving me the stare of death.

"Hit me up, Max. We are going out too; maybe we can hang," Britt entices.

"Definitely."

We leave the restaurant. I want nothing more than to go home. I am not sure I can endure more of Max and his endless appetite for hunting women. It's relentless, and I don't begrudge it for him; I'm just not in wingman mode. I'm in "fuck off all of humanity" mode.

"Shep, what's with the cock block?"

"Dude, you got her number, didn't you?"

"Well, yeah."

"Then no blocking of the cock. Twenty dollars says she is blowing you later."

"I'd like that," Max groans.

If there is such thing as the blow job queen, then my boy is the BJ king. Most guys like to brag as to how many women they have had intercourse with. But Maxie? Nope. He is all about the oral, and then he rates them, mostly by degree of difficulty. Max loves the old drive-and-suck. Gotta love the classics. I don't know how one can concentrate and properly enjoy the act under such auspices, but everyone has their skill set, right?

"I'm sure you would." I pause. "Dude, you care if I bail? I am not much feeling the social scene."

"Dude! First the cock block and now the wingman block! You are being a dick, Shep!"

"Yeah, man, I know, but you don't need me, and I need some space from humanity."

Max puts his hand on my shoulder. "OK, Shep, I'm sorry. Drop me off downtown? My car is down there, anyway, so I don't have to Uber after I go out."

"You should Uber, Max; drinking, driving, and getting sucked off is a bad combo."

"Not in my experience!" he says, laughing his ass off.

I drop Max off and head home. As soon as he is gone, I feel that pang of loneliness that I abhor. Still, it is way better than being annoyed by a bunch of people I don't really know or want to know. Life is a lonely place, so be it.

I do wonder about Aria. I should be responsible, but then I get angry at myself for thinking that. She should have been responsible and not done drugs. I'm not saying that would have made me ready to be a father—it wouldn't have—but I sure as shit would have felt more guilty.

I get home and crawl into bed alone on a Saturday night.

THIRTEEN

Sunday, I decide to hike in a local park. I am alone again. The last time I went for a sojourn in the woods, I was with Aria. It makes me pretty miserable. I am OK with being alone, or at least that is what I tell myself until I actually am. When you are surrounded by people most of the time, it is easy to long for solitude, until that becomes reality.

Technically, I am not alone. There are other hikers, dog walkers, and mountain bikers. Chances are I know some of them, but I have opted to bring headphones and sunglasses, the ultimate cover for saying "fuck off" without uttering a word.

During the hike, I find myself checking my phone, which annoys me. I want to hear from

Aria, if for no other reason to know how she is. I wish I didn't care; I shouldn't, but I do. Funny, when it comes down to it, I believe men are way more sensitive than women, or maybe it's a gender anomaly, or there is no rhyme or reason to how people are regardless of sex?

Aria is radio silent. I have no clue what to do. Part of me thinks I should subdue my anger with her and the drugs; maybe it was a one-time thing? The woman is carrying my child, but then it occurs to me that if she was doing drugs without me knowing, she could she be fucking someone else, and I wouldn't have known. Yes, I am that insecure. I have been cheated on before. I get hit on by women who know that I know their boyfriends or husbands. It's sick, and I am not a fan. I just never understood the point of cheating; it's hurtful. Why take that risk of someone you have been so intimately involved with? Yet it happens all the time. I wish the thought had never crossed my mind. Would she do that? Maybe to distract me from the drug issue? Ugh!

Dude! Max was in a car accident! In the Hospital. No Bueno

The text comes in from Bennie.

I stare at the phone, incredulous; I am paralyzed by the news. I call Ben immediately. He doesn't pick up.

LMK what is happening. I am on my way to Elmwood Gen.

No response. I break into a run so I can get to my car as fast as possible. In my head I do the rewind of the previous night. I feel guilty for not taking his keys. All I can think of is that as a human being, I am slipping down the decency scale at an epic pace. First Aria, now Max, and I feel responsible for both.

I get to the hospital. Max's mom and sister are huddled together on a waiting-room sofa. Bennie is leaning against the wall next to him, staring at his phone, vleeping.

"I got here as soon as I heard. Is Max OK?"

Max's relatives stay huddled. They don't even look at me. It throws me. Bennie stops staring at his phone and grabs me by the arm.

"It's not good."

"What the fuck does 'not good' mean?"

"The girl he was with is dead, Shep, and Max is in critical condition. I think they are on a second surgery."

"Fuck." I can't believe it. "What girl?"

"I dunno, Britt something."

"Fuck, fuck, fuck, fuck! He met her last night at Chow's. For fuck's sake he was probably getting a blow job! That stupid fuck!"

"Well, if you are gunna go, Shep—"

"Really, Ben? Asshole."

"Weren't you with him last night?"

"What are you saying, Bennie?"

"That you could have looked out for him?"

I must be giving Ben the look of death; it feels as if my stare is searing his soul. I can tell it's bad, because he actually looks fearful of me.

"You think this happened because I didn't babysit him? I can't take the blame for this." I walk off.

"He texted me last night, after you left; Max didn't follow why you wouldn't stay with him."

I turn and storm back to Bennie. "I have my own shit going on is why, not that I need to explain it to you!"

I know I should stay, but I am feeling like I might act out on Ben. Before I leave, I turn to Max's family and say hello and how sorry I am. The guilt of what has happened weighs on and probably would have even if Bennie hadn't said something.

FOURTEEN

I am checked out. I am working and physically at Insane! Fitness, but truthfully, I am not there at all. I'm not sure it matters. I am training with Brandon, and even though he was on time, the level of effort he is putting in is less than inspired. He doesn't seem to mind that I am not all there; in fact, he seems to be encouraged.

"I'm cashed," Brandon announces.

I stand there cross-armed and nod. The guy looks at me for a moment, clearly surprised I have gone mute on him. It appears as if he may try to get some chatter out of me but then thinks better of it and simply walks away.

I breathe a sigh of relief. I know that I should not be working, although I cannot say where I should be. My gut is to be in bed safely kept under a mountain of covers. In fact, I am fully planning on that and avoiding Rack's useless weekly meeting. I don't even need an excuse to skip, because if it comes up, I am going to play the "my friend is on death's door" card.

As I come down the stairs, I stop dead because I see something I do not expect to see: Aria. She is talking to Michael, who is probably also contemplating using Max as an excuse to avoid more of Rack's weekly bullshit. Aria sees me, and Michael looks up; he says good-bye, and she waves at me.

My head swims as I descend the stair. I really can't deal with this now, but I may not be able to deal with this ever. "Hey," Aria says softly. "Can we talk?"

I nod. "I was on my way home. Meet me there?"

"Shep, I'd rather not. Maybe just the coffee place?"

"I just have to grab my stuff."

We walk around the corner to the Starbucks. She buys me a coffee and herself a tea, and we sit in the least densely populated area of the chain.

"I'm sorry about the other day. I know that disappointed you, Shep."

"It's your body, Aria, not my place to judge. I just don't want to be around it."

She nods. "I've been having a hard time and using it as an escape. It didn't start out that way."

"I don't think it ever does."

She nods again.

"Look, you don't owe me anything, Aria."

"I thought an explanation was in order, not that it was much of one." She pauses. "I'm going to Planned Parenthood next week."

"OK."

"I'm not going to keep it."

I feel a tremendous conflict as the words leave her lips and land in my ears with a bizarre crash. On the one hand, there is relief but on the other a sorrow of tragic proportions. I can see she is suffering with it. I soften.

"I'm sorry."

"You shouldn't be. It isn't what you signed on for, and neither did I. I would be afraid to have the baby, anyway, even if we had planned it, which we clearly did not."

"I will go with you."

"I don't want you to, Shep. I need to do this alone. I can't see a scenario where we work, so I wanted to say good-bye. I'm going to move to Florida."

I just look at her. Like the other news of the day, it comes with a heavy heart. "Florida?"

"Yeah, Florida. I have a cousin down there, and she just lost a roommate. She thinks she can get me some bartending gigs too."

I bow my head, and Aria reaches out and touches my hand.

"You OK?" she asks.

"Just seems like my life is being turned upside down. It feels like pure chaos."

"Yeah, I know the feeling, Shep. I didn't come to the decision lightly. I didn't think you would rebound from what has happened in the last few days. I'm beyond hormonal and may not be making rational decisions, but I did feel at the least I tore the soul out of us, and I don't want to be here if it can't be with you."

I look at her as I fight off tears. I don't want her to leave, but I know that she really should.

"It's not that bad, Aria; the drugs really bothered me, the pregnancy not as much. It just wasn't what I was expecting. If we could establish some steady ground, I think we would be great parents."

Aria looks at me; she is unsuccessful at holding off the tears. Finally, she says, "Maybe someday, Shep. Maybe someday."

Aria gets up and kisses me on the mouth. It is the final good-bye, and in that moment, I know that someday will never come.

FIFTEEN

I sit at the bar alone. It isn't as if I have much of a choice. I have no girlfriend anymore, and of the two buddies I call my best friends, one is in a coma, and the other seems to believe I had a heavy hand in getting him in said state. Sure, I have other so-called friends, but those are of the fair-weather variety, and I need someone substantial, or no one at all.

I could have asked a number of women out with me, too. I am lucky and know a lot of them who would provide company of various levels, but same as with the friends, I need some substance.

That currently takes the form of vodka. It isn't a friend or a conquest, but it doesn't talk and doesn't want shit from me except for me to consume it. Me and the vodka are vibing.

It's early, and a Tuesday to boot, so not so many other patrons are getting their drunk on. I sit with my head down, staring into my clear libation, wishing my conscious felt that pure. I wonder if Aria is testing me. Does she want me to stop her? Protest the leaving? There is a part of me that doesn't want to let go. The thought of us apart makes me ill, like there is poison coursing through my veins and directly into my soul. Yet, there is another part of me that can't deal with whatever she is doing to herself. The drugs seriously bother me, to the point I doubt I could ever trust her. In the end, letting her go is the best thing.

Some paramedics come into the bar and saddle up next to me. I don't move other than to order another vodka. I don't really drink much, but this feels like a special occasion. The paramedics are clearly off a day's work. They seem both sullen and happy to be away from the grind. One knocks into me as he sits down. I turn and look. The guy looks back at me as if I have done something wrong.

"Shep, why don't you give me your keys?" the bartender suggests.

I look at the guy. I went to high school with him, but for the life of me, I cannot remember the dude's name. Art? Or did I know him from art class? Ugh, the Grey Goose is having an effect. I hand him my keys.

"A wise choice," one of the paramedics chimes in.

I look at him.

"A lot of our business comes from drunk driving. We had two last night. Some guy got his cock gnarled getting a blow job. Girl didn't make it. The guy, I dunno. It wasn't good."

I can feel my blood boiling with an assist from the Goose.

"Can you imagine dying with a dick in your mouth?" the other medic wonders aloud.

"I bet you guys can," I snap.

"What the fuck!" the one who ran into me says, standing.

"Guys!" Art, or whatever the bartender's name is, says.

The paramedics look surprised at the bartender's aggressive tone.

"We know the person you are talking about," he tells them.

"Oh, sorry," one capitulates.

They sit back down. I do nothing but stare into my glass.

"You're welcome, Shep."

"Just keep the glass wet."

He pours me another drink, and I can feel his eyes searing on me despite the fact I am not looking at him.

SIXTEEN

I wake up in bed. I quickly realize that it isn't mine. I sit up as fast as I can, which turns out to be a bad idea, because I am really, really hungover. I quickly lose my bearings, but before I do, I feel like I am somewhere I have been before.

"You are gunna want these," a familiar female voice says.

I vaguely see a hand with some pills. I follow the hand to the body and face it belongs to. She is blurry, but I know who it is.

"Come on, Shep; take the aspirin," Jenna says, handing me the glass of water first.

I swallow the pills and inhale the water so quickly, it is a wonder that I don't drown.

"Jenna?"

"Jesus, you don't remember, do you?"

I grab my head as my bearings slowly return. I look around the room, as it becomes unblurred. Clothes are strewn about, mine and hers. She is wearing a T-shirt I recognize as the one I distantly recall wearing at the bar.

"Did we?"

"Yup!" Jenna confirms with certain glee.

"Shit. Did I at least use a condom?"

"Nope!"

"Ugh, did I…"

"I don't think so."

"You don't think…"

"Shep, I was pretty lit too, just not as much as you. Don't worry; I downed a morning-after pill."

I fall back into the mattress. It feels like all the jackhammers of the world are pounding away inside my head. Jenna's voice is shrill and annoying. I want to leave, but aside from all the jackhammering, I'm not sure I can stand.

Jenna sits down next to me and tousles my hair. It feels amazing. I try to imagine Aria, although I don't know why. I guess despite the fact I had senseless unprotected sex with another woman, Aria is still in my heart.

"I could spoil you, Shep; it seems like you could use it."

"Why would you say that?"

"Seriously, dude? How fucked up were you? And alone? It adds up pretty much only one way."

"That obvious?" I ask, opening my eyes.

Jenna nods. "It's OK, Shep. I'm here."

"Thank you. I'm not sure I am in a place to be much of anything to anyone right now. I don't want to mislead you."

"If you are trying to scare me off, it isn't working. My offer to spoil you stands, no strings."

I look into her eyes; they seem to be filled with love. Maybe she is right; I could use it. Jenna touches my face and gets up. She walks into the kitchen area, swaying her bare ass that peeks out from under my T-shirt. I can see that she is pouring coffee into mugs. She brings one to me, smiling as she does.

I take the mug and sip. I realize she has made it just how I like, without asking. It is heaven sent. I can feel my headache abating with every taste.

"Do you want to fuck me again now or after breakfast?"

I feel my cock growing under the sheets.

"Oh! It looks like you are ready now! Great," she says, taking off the shirt.

I take another sip of the coffee and put it on the nightstand. Jenna throws back the sheet and wastes no time taking me in her mouth. It's a little sloppy, but I am turned on that she is sucking my dick. I hold her head down, making her swallow all of me, until she gags and comes up for air. I expertly flip her on her stomach and fuck her from behind. It seems familiar; I wonder if we did it doggie the night before too.

"Come inside me!"

The idea of her asking this almost makes me come instantly, but I hold off. I pull her hair and tell her to beg harder for it. She does, and it is as if this whole master-and-servant deal is kismet. I can no longer hold back, and I explode inside her. I feel as if I yell really loud so that her entire apartment building knows I just had an earth-shattering orgasm.

"That was nice," Jenna says. "You must be hungry—egg time."

I collapse on the bed as Jenna cooks. She turns on some music and sashays about the small kitchen, periodically looking at me as if for some kind of approval. The looks make me nervous; she seems all in love. It isn't what I need, yet at the same time, she *is* exactly what the doctor ordered. I rationalize that I have told her where I stand and that if she goes down the fucked-up Shep rabbit hole, then it's on her.

Jenna brings me bacon and eggs in bed, on a tray that neatly unfolds on my lap. I have to admit I do like the spoiling she has promised and is delivering on. Maybe this can work? Whatever, it's functional now. That's all that matters.

I destroy the food. It's a hangover cure, or at least hangover help. I know I should probably leave, but I really just want to nap it out and maybe fuck some more.

"Is it cool if I crash a bit?" I ask.

A massive smile slips across Jena's face. "Cuddle time!"

"Uh...OK," I say with trepidation.

"I'm just gunna clean up, and I will be right back! Maybe a nice massage to help you knock off?"

I nod. I know I shouldn't like it. I should definitely leave. Maybe it's OK that I do like it. Maybe I should stay. Maybe it's OK to let her do this. How can I deny her what she wants, especially when it's no skin off my back?

SEVENTEEN

Max's sister has been texting to keep me posted, since I am not on speaking terms with Bennie. The update is that there is no update. My lifelong buddy is in a coma, and even if he does wake up, they seem pretty sure that he will have shitty quality of life. The doctors have said that he will likely be paralyzed from the neck down, have limited speech, and require care around the clock. It's horrible to think, but I don't wish that life for him. If he dies, he at least enjoyed his time while he was here, brief as it was. Beyond any of that, is misery.

I feel bad for not going back to the hospital, but I can't bring myself to. It is selfish, especially toward Max's family. The truth is, I can't handle it right now, and there is little I could do even if I was feeling more stable. I don't want to run into Ben, and I don't want to see Max like this. I prefer to remember him intact and alive, even if that really isn't the way it is.

I don't want to work, but I figure that I should in order not to completely deflate into a bedridden depressive. I go in early to try and take my many frustrations out on the weights. The lights are on again, when they shouldn't be. I use my key to get into Insane! Fitness and lock up behind me. Once inside, I head to the lockers, and as I am about to enter, one of the janitors comes barreling out, almost knocking me over.

"Hey!" a voice comes behind him.

Rack comes running after the janitor, whose name I cannot conjure.

"Fuck, Julio," Rack says.

"I'm sorry," Julio apologizes to me, flitting his eyes at Rack.

"Just get back to work!" Rack commands.

Julio looks at Rack, almost hurt, before scurrying off.

"Sorry, Shep, fucking Mexicans."

"I think I've heard him say he is from Costa Rica."

"Whatever. You about to train?"

"Yeah."

"Have a good workout," he says, wiping unexplained sweat from his forehead.

I nod and drop my stuff in my locker. Upstairs I see Julio cleaning windows about as far from me as humanly possible. I don't want to know what they were up to, although I can imagine. I blast music, train in the virtually empty gym, and then shower. It is a bit before

5:00 a.m., and I crave a drink. I guzzle protein, wishing it were hard liquor. I have never been a big drinker, and I know I am in the shit right now. I miss Aria. I miss Max. Two huge cogs in my wheel of life, and I will never have either of them back.

I kill my shake and put on my game face. It isn't uncommon for me to wear fake like an old friend—hazard of the service industry, I assume. It is exhausting to be "on" for an entire day, let alone several in a row. I am in for a battle, and I know it.

I have a new client first, although she may not be a client at all. Insane! Fitness sucks people into buying sessions by giving out a freebie when they initially join. All I know is that her name is Mandy. I wait at the front desk, waiting for her to sign in. I abhor trying to train a client cold. I want to leave and get drunk, but I talk myself down off that ledge. I have a full morning. Distraction is key.

Mandy appears to be a no-show. I get paid regardless, but it is still annoying. I could be doing something else, not even a call from her or some sort of heads-up. Eh, it's free money. I just stand and wait at the front. The nice thing about the early-morning crowd is that they are serious about their workouts. They come in before their daily life begins, they train, they go. It isn't too social. I am thankful because I would prefer life if I didn't have to deal with a soul.

A woman comes in through the doors. I perk up immediately, as I do not know her, but sure as shit, I want to. I can only hope that this is Mandy.

She continues to stare at her phone as she approaches the front. I catch myself standing up straighter and puff out my chest. She is about five foot seven and absolutely stunning. Her long brown hair cascades down her shoulders, and it seems as if there is not a single hair out of place. She is dressed in all black, a form-fitting top and yoga pants, which makes me certain that if this is indeed my client, she has no real need for a trainer at all. I make her mid to late twenties, my age range. In a word she is amazing, and I cannot take my eyes off her. Some poor sap coming in behind her practically trips over himself ogling her. She may be in the top three women ever to enter the gym. Finally, she looks up. I smile. She looks at me as if she wonders if I am relevant in her orbit.

"Uh, hey. I'm supposed to be training with Shoop or something."

"Shep—you are training with Shep. That's me. You must be Mandy."

She looks down at her phone as if she hopes it will save her from the awkwardness. It doesn't.

"Cool," she says.

"Cool."

"Is there a locker room where I can drop my things?"

"There is, but we have a small problem."

"We do?"

Mandy asks it in such a painful manner, I half wonder if I was telling the truth.

"We were scheduled for five. I have a client at five thirty; it's five twenty now."

"So, you are saying I wasted my time coming down here, Shoop?"

"It's Shep, Mandy. No, I am not saying that at all. We can discuss your goals and make another appointment."

"Yeah, but I am here now."

"And I am glad you made it. I just wish you had been able to get here when our appointment started."

"Dude, you are being a dick."

I take a deep breath.

"I'm sorry you feel that way, Mandy, but this is my job. I get paid per client. When I train people here, often they go back to back, like today, like now."

"You do home training too?"

"Sometimes."

"Good, then can we set that up? Like a two-hour window so I don't waste my time again?"

"Sure."

"Give me your phone."

I hand Mandy my cell. She expertly punches in her number and texts herself so she has my information.

"Can you train me tonight? I get done with work at eight."

"I will make it work."

She smiles at me, as if I am just another man conquered. I couldn't care less. She can conquer me all she likes. I watch her as she leaves. Mandy looks phenomenal coming and going.

EIGHTEEN

I enter my house to see my mother staring at the wall. There is half a bottle of cheap vodka, cap off, next to a coffee mug. She gets like this sometimes, depressed. I can't say I blame her, although sometimes the causes of her pain are not the most reasonable.

I am pretty sure she has positioned herself so I would find her like this. I could really use not dealing with anyone else's baggage right now, but it is my mother, so I hope that distracting myself with whatever is on her mind will relieve me of what is going on in my world.

"Mom?"

She just keeps staring. I put a hand on her shoulder. She looks at me slowly; it is beyond alarming. It is as if I am a stranger to her.

"You OK?"

"Shep…"

"Yeah, Ma?"

"Aria came by today."

"She did?"

"I didn't know."

I sigh. I have never made it a habit to keep my parents in the loop as to what is going on in my love life, although Aria and my mother were thick as thieves. It was both lovely and daunting all at once. For sure, you hope that your family accepts and likes your partner, but there is an awkward line than can be crossed when they become friends as well.

"I never told you that I had an abortion. Before I met your father. I was too young, and I knew it. I never told the boy. Now that I think of it, I'm not sure I knew how to even contact him."

I wonder if I am more shocked that Aria spilled to my mother about being pregnant or my mom spilling about her situation. I feel sick with guilt.

"Mom, she really shouldn't have said anything."

"Why not? She is suffering with it. You have no idea what a woman deals with, and she trusts me. I am glad she said something."

"Sure, I can see how happy you are with the booze, at noon, on a weekday."

"It's never going to leave her, Luke. Aria will carry guilt with her for the rest of her life."

"I can't imagine what it will be like, but we didn't plan this; we aren't ready for this. We have other issues too, Ma. It all sort of snowballed—no, avalanched—at once. I can't, in good conscience, start a family under these circumstances. There is a third person involved."

"Sure, Luke. That's rational, but what I am feeling now, thirty-five years after the fact, is as if it happened yesterday. Common sense has nothing to do with it."

"You don't know the entire story. We were breaking up without this, and even if we weren't, the solution would probably be the same. She made the choice on her own. I didn't even say anything, but I do agree with Aria. Did she tell you she was moving?"

"Yeah, she did. You want a drink?"

I do. I desperately do. I want something to wash away all the pain I feel accruing in my soul. I also know that it is a dangerous road to tread. I see my mother marinating her sadness in epic proportion, fueled, in part, by cheap midday vodka.

"No. I want to try and rest, maybe get my head on."

"What will you do about Aria?"

"There is nothing to do; she is moving. Maybe it's time I am actually single for a while instead of continuously latching on to temporary partners."

My mother says nothing; she simply sips at her mug of booze, as if she is a babe, suckling nourishment. It is downright scary, but I have no clue as to what to do.

"You OK by yourself? I want to shower and put my head down."

Mom nods. I leave her with trepidation.

"Luke?"

"Yeah?"

"You know a girl named Jenna?"

"Uh-huh. Why?"

"She stopped by. I think she baked cookies. I left them in your room."

NINETEEN

Rack grabs me on the way in for my afternoon and evening clients. He is sweating profusely despite being dressed in his sales clothes.

"Shep, what the fuck is happening?"

Rack is jittery, and I look at him as if he is out of his mind.

"Why are you asking that?"

"Your numbers are down this week. I've had complaints that you have been canceling on clients."

"Yeah, Rack, that's right. My best friend is paralyzed and in a coma; he will likely not come out of, and Aria and I are done. Am I not allowed to go through some shit and take some time to myself?"

"Not if you want to keep this job."

I look at Rack, incredulous.

"I'm your most popular trainer, Rack; you seriously want to fuck with me?"

"I can get by with Ezra and Lucy," he tells me matter-of-factly.

"Oh yeah?"

"Yeah."

Rack gets in my face. He is sweating profusely, as if he is in a sauna. I don't take my eyes off him, but it is getting to be prime hours, and the scene we are creating isn't exactly private. I feel eyes on us, lots of them.

"You're coked up, aren't you?" I ask.

"I don't do drugs," Rack says loud enough for everyone to hear.

"Sure, you don't."

Rack boils over and pushes me pretty hard, which makes me snap. I lunge at him, catching him in the face with my fist. It takes him by surprise and knocks him over. I am about to finish the job, fueled by the rage of all the shit I've been dealing with, but I don't make it. Ezra comes flying in, putting his massive body between Rack and me.

"You're done here, Shep!" Rack says, picking himself up off the floor.

"Don't feed into it, man; walk away," Ezra advises.

Ezra lets me go. I look at Rack. He looks at me. I sense the fear in his eyes, and so I snigger.

"One of you should take the night off. Aren't you done for the day, Rack?" Ezra, the voice of reason, asks.

Rack just nods and walks out the door.

"He is totally on drugs," Ezra says to me. "What an asshole."

"Yep."

The crowd that had gathered to watch the drama unfold dissipates. And I head upstairs for my first client, wishing I had been fired. I just don't want to be here.

The gym is packed. Par for the course in prime hours. I am vaguely distracted by the copious amount of attractive women, most of whom I know or have some rapport with just based on familiarity alone.

Come fuck me.

The text comes from Jenna, along with a picture of she and I doing it. I do not remember her filming us, so I can only assume that this was taken in my vodka haze.

Working.

Then another sext, her striking a seductive pose in a mirror, naked.

Lucy, who is training someone next to me, sees the shot on my phone.

"Jesus, Shep."

I look at her blankly.

"Put it away," she says finally.

I nod. I can see the sympathy in her eyes. I pocket the phone and resume sleeping through my session. I perk up considerably when Lucy gives my ass a squeeze as she walks by. I smile at her, and she smiles back.

Lucy and I fuck in her car in the lot of the gym. The irony isn't lost on me that she was calling me out for being unprofessional, when clearly any latecomers to Insane! Fitness will know what is happening if they can see through the fogged windows. Lucy is the third woman I have had unprotected sex with in almost as many days. I come inside her too, crying out in a combination of both pain and ecstasy all in one sound. What am I doing? Trying to impregnate the entire town?

"I've wanted to do that for a while, Shep."

"Yeah, me too," I lie.

"It's not going to happen again," she says.

"Whatever, Lucy."

"Get the fuck out of my car."

I manage to get my sweats back up from around my ankles and exit her car. She doesn't even look at me as she drives off.

"What the fuck was that?" I ask out loud.

"Women, about as predictable as a fart in a hurricane."

I turn around and see Michael. He has a shit-eating grin on his face, and if I am not mistaken, one hell of a hard-on.

"How long you been there?"

"Long enough for my dick to get hard, which at my age isn't a quick operation."

"How old are you again? Wait, aren't you Father Time's great-grandfather or something?"

"Something like that, Shep. Don't worry; age will come for you too if your dick doesn't fall off first, from whatever she just gave you."

"You saying she gets around?"

"I'm saying you aren't the first one I've seen get out of her car with jizz on his pants."

"Good to know." I chuckle.

"Don't get me wrong, kid; I would accept an invite into that car of hers any day."

"Have a good night, man," I say, walking away.

"Disinfect that cock, Shep, if you ever want to use it again."

I give him the finger without looking back, but I am sure he is actually right.

TWENTY

My mother is sitting in the kitchen staring with the vodka again. The only light she has is the one coming from the vent oven lights, one of which has fizzled out.

"Jesus, Ma."

She barely registers my existence, other than to push the bottle my way. I think about it and justify that it is at least nighttime. I grab the bottle and have a swig out of it, and as I do, I realize that my mother and I are genetically depressive, perhaps with a side of alcoholism.

"Luke, she left you an envelope."

"Aria? She came by again?"

"Yeah, I guess she was on her way out of town. Like you said, she is headed to Tampa."

You gunna come fuck me or what?

Jenna. I *am* going to fuck her. I *am* going to solve my problems with sex and booze.

Just got hm, gunna shower, will meet you out, long day.

Kool

She sends me another crotch shot, lips spread with her fingers.

"Who is that?"

"A client...er...I dunno, I am meeting some friends out."

"You have some weed? I didn't want to go through your shit, Luke, but I want so desperately to be numb."

My mother starts to cry. It breaks my soul to see her like this, but I get it, because the reasons may not be the same, but we sure as shit share the same misery. I stand up and put my arms around her. She holds on to me as if her life depended on it.

"It happened almost thirty years ago. I still can't forgive myself."

"You have to find a way."

She looks up at me and nods. It's as if she just needed someone to tell her this; either that or she is appeasing me with a white lie.

"You going to be OK?"

"Yeah," she says, patting my hand. "Go on now; I know you want to go out."

"I can stay."

"No, I'm going to go to bed."

"Can you talk to someone? Dad?"

My mother gets up, places a gentle hand on my shoulder, kisses my cheek, and shuffles off. I hear her ascend the stairs to her bedroom. The sobbing is muted but crushes my soul no less.

TWENTY-ONE

Jenna picks me up wearing a tight red dress. It may be the weed talking, but she looks sorta hot. I have her drive because I plan on getting really, really lit. I already smoked a bit too much; excess seems to be my first, last, and middle name these days. Maybe it's the guilt I feel for fucking Lucy, or maybe it's just because my self-worth is in the shitter, or maybe I just don't like myself very much anymore. Perhaps I never did.

I still plan on excess, despite the fact I am aware of it. I just don't care. I am surprised I didn't drive, maybe in the secret hope of crashing into a tree, but Max's accident isn't lost on me. I may not care so much about myself right now, but I saw what that did to his family and friends. I may be acting like a selfish, carefree prick, but I have to draw the line somewhere.

We go to a shit hole of a Mexican restaurant that is really a bar called Sancho's. The place smells as though stale beer has seeped into the floor and then been urinated on. It isn't packed like I expected, but it isn't empty either. I see so many people I know from either growing up in Elmwood or others who train at Insane! I feel as if I loathe them all.

Jenna walks behind me like some dutiful geisha as I beeline to the bar. There are a lot of women there, and they all smile and wave as if I am the pick of the litter. It makes me feel good, but then I always have gotten my validation from women. I am also feeling like I want to use sex and booze as coping mechanisms. Despite the fact that Jenna, dutiful and willing, is just steps behind me, I am eye-fucking half the bar and wondering how many of these women I can have. If I weren't high and ready to get blind drunk, I might realize that I am going off the deep end. I, for lack of a better word, have become as indifferent as indifferent can be.

I sidle up to the bar, and as I do, I realize that I haven't eaten. Then, par for the course, I realize I don't care. I will get hammered faster this way.

"Tequila, whatever the house stuff is," I ask the bartender.

Jenna looks at me sort of sideways.

"Yeah?"

"You aren't even going to ask what I want?" she asks hang-doggedly.

"I thought you were meeting friends or something?"

"Yeah, I guess, but I came here with you."

I should feel bad, but truth is, all I want to feel is more numb. Then, what I feel is angry. Rack is in the house. He is with his girlfriend. I am still pissed he came at me the way he did. He sees me and waves as if nothing has happened. Maybe I should just let it go. I wave back, but inside my rage festers. It isn't necessarily because of Rack, but he seems to be a natural target given recent events.

"Isn't that your boss?"

I don't respond to Jenna. I am resentful toward her too. The resentment is borne out of the fact she is trying to love me. How can anyone love someone who clearly hates himself?

"I think we should have a three-way," I come up with.

Jenna looks at me as if assessing my seriousness. I return the stare with as much seriousness someone as lifted as I am can muster. It seems to take.

"I've never done that."

"Sure, and you don't have to. It's just I'm in this place, where I dunno, I just need to fuck as many women as possible. I can do it with or without you. I've always wanted a girlfriend who was cool with picking up women with me. I guess that's just not you."

"No, no, Shep, I didn't say I wouldn't. I just said I hadn't. Truth is, I would let you do anything you want to me."

Jackpot. It's always a double-edged sword when someone speaks those words, but now all I can think of is Jenna and girl number two.

"That's sweet. Why don't you get that ball rolling and I will get you a margarita?"

"Tonight?"

"Yeah, tonight."

Jenna seems hesitant.

"Problem? I thought you just said you were OK with it. Totally cool if you aren't. I get it; I couldn't share someone with another guy."

"No, no, no. We can. I will probably need to get pretty hammered."

"That's what we came for, isn't it?"

"I came to be with you."

"Right, yeah, of course, but since we are here, and we both want to do this..."

"I need a drink," she says. "Desperately."

The bartender does return, and I ask her for shots. I slug half the tequila she has brought and offer the rest to Jenna, who looks at me as if I just proposed, when all I am wondering is what other filth I can make her do if I just get her fucked up enough.

"Thanks," she says, smiling seductively.

"So why don't you introduce me to your friends? We can decide which ones we are going to fuck."

"Shep, I'm not sure if they would go for that."

I nod with a sense of as much disappointment as I can channel. Our shots come, and we down them fast. I ask for another round.

"It's cool if you aren't into it. That's the feeling I get, but I really want to have a three-way. It just feels like the thing to do."

"You have done it before?"

"A couple of times, with a girlfriend mostly, not Aria; she was against it, and I resented her."

"I want to give you what you want, Shep; I think I'm falling for you."

I pretend not to hear the last bit; instead I acknowledge some people I know. As it turns out, Rack and his girlfriend come over to say hello to the same people.

"Shep, I'm sorry about what happened," Rack says. "Lemme buy you a drink."

I nod. Rack and I move to the bar. I am wearing a nice buzz that lies in between baked and drunk, a perfect combination of both, not too much or too little of either the high or the low. I wonder if that has calmed me. I appreciate that he has apologized.

"What are you drinking, tequila?"

"Yeah, that would be great."

Rack flags down the bartender and orders us shots, and as he does, he not so discreetly hands her some cash, clearly not meant for drinks. Rack is beefed up; I honestly don't know how he toes the line between hard drugs and steroids.

"I know you have been through a bunch of shit lately. I should have been more sensitive," he tells me. "You punch like my mom, though."

I laugh, now edging more toward drunk rather than high. I no longer hate him the way I did when we first got to the place. I actually sort of like him. I guess I always have. Aside from the nagging meetings he insists we sit through weekly, he leaves me alone. I try not to judge his lifestyle; it wouldn't be my choice, but I have no right to judge anyone else these days.

"So," Rack says matter-of-factly, "are you ready?"

"For what?"

"To go down the rabbit hole."

"The what?"

"Are you too young to get the reference? I thought Alice in Wonderland was universally known."

"Oh yeah, I know it, but what does that have to do with me?"

Rack puts his hand on my shoulder. "You want to know why I was so fucked up the other day?"

Drugs? I shake my head.

"I hadn't been."

"Been?"

"Exactly."

"Rack, I appreciate the apology, but this is getting super weird. I just wanna get hammered and meet some women," I say, getting up.

"No! You don't understand," he says with urgency.

It is an odd moment to be sure, one where you sense somehow that something important is happening, yet it really shouldn't be anything. It's the funky opaque world between perception and instinct, a crossroads.

"What the fuck are you talking about, Rack?"

"Aha! The billion-dollar question!"

I stare at him, wondering if I should just punch him again. He grins like the Cheshire cat. "Come with me."

I want to move away from Rack; his eyes seem to be black like saucers, yet something inside me says to trust him on this. I realize that I am nodding. The grin becomes impossibly wider, and Rack takes me by the arm, and we plow through the crowd to an exit door, leading us outside to an alleyway. It is odd how the crowd seems to effortlessly part for us as we get out.

We burst into the alley that I never knew was there. Cool, delicious, air fills my grateful lungs, and I feel alive. Something is different, although I cannot say what.

The alley has bright yellow bricks, which may have been imported from Oz. The bricks have a sheen to them, as if they have been recently polished. It is astonishing in a way, as alleyways are usually reserved for dumpsters and riffraff. This place is shiny. It feels happy. Then it gets weird. Rack stops as the door to the bar closes. He turns to me. We are too close, yet I cannot move.

"Kiss me," he suggests.

"Dude, no judgment here, but I'm not into that sort of thing."

"It's the only way it works."

"For you, maybe. I like chicks, Rack. Don't you have a girlfriend?"

"It's not for a homosexual purpose, Shep."

"Seems pretty clear that it is," I say, turning back to the door that has no handle to reopen.

"Taste the rainbow, Shep," Rack says, turning me around and showing me a small rainbow candy on his tongue.

I want to protest, but as if the universe wants me to kiss my first man, and for some unknown reason, I capitulate. I open my mouth and take Rack's rainbow-candied kiss. It is brief but oddly gentle and less awkward than I thought. The candy is passed to me in the embrace, and it sits on my tongue, dispersing flavor in my mouth that I could never describe. Only to say that it feels as if I am tasting the culmination of every delicious thing I have ever consumed.

Someone in a rabbit suit actually hops by, stopping at the sight of Rack. There is a staring contest, Rack looking into the black obsidian pools that represent the rabbit's eyes. The person inside the costume says something, but interference from the head makes it inaudible. Rack shakes his head. The rabbit cocks his.

"Wait, you too?" Rack guesses.

The rabbit nods and takes off the head portion. Inside the costume is Julio, the janitor from the gym. The stare-down continues, eye to human eye this time. He looks at me, and as he does, a slick smile slides across his face.

"Got yourself some rainbow, huh?"

I nod. He nods, and then he jumps on Rack like a sailor's girlfriend seeing her man for the first time since he last shipped off. It seems he wanted some rainbow action of his own. For a truly bizarre situation, it has an oddly normal feel. Everything is off, yet nothing really is. *Or is it*? I feel fascinated by these two men I know from one world, yet clearly not at all in another. Then I realize that I may not know myself. They finally break. Julio shows me his tongue; he has three rainbow candies on his.

"I've built up a tolerance," he explains.

"He has," Rack chimes in.

"I've got a vent in the back of this thing," Julio informs us, turning around.

Rack looks at me, eyebrows raised Jack Nicholson style. There is a vent. Rack lifts it, revealing Julio's bare ass.

"You wanna go first?" Rack asks me.

"I'm good on that."

"Suit yourself," Rack says, unzipping himself.

I definitely do not want to stay for this. I want out of the yellow-bricked alleyway. I start to say good-bye to Rack and Julio, but they have already started. I look briefly as the beefy Rack pounds away at a man in a rabbit suit. Fortunately, I have the good sense to get out of there.

Rack and Julio occupy what seems to be the end of the alley. Although I can see no wall, there is a distinctive darkness at one end that may as well have a "keep out" sign written in blood, dangling just before the abyss. It has a sinister sensibility that scares the shit out of me. Perhaps it is the contrast to the glow of the bricks, or maybe it is the combination of booze, weed, and whatever rainbow does to you.

I opt for the well-lit way through the golden alley. I want to get back into Sancho's. I expect a door but find none. All that I see, is a golden-bricked alley.

I keep walking. It feels great, and the air is cool on my face. It is as if the breeze is soothing me intentionally. I wish I could strip off all my clothes and allow my entire body to taste the kiss of the wind on my skin.

The alley seems infinite and devoid of any souls. Finally, I stop and sit, weary from the walking. I wonder where everyone is. I wonder where I am. I begin to fill with an epic sadness, like a balloon slowly being filled with helium; the sadness stretches my soul until it seems I may just burst.

The weight of my life seems to be sinking me, like a stone, weighted by bigger and heavier stones. The depression deepens to hideous depths. I feel, in that moment, that if I died in the moment, I would be relieved.

"Shep!"

I look up. I can't believe what I am seeing. It is Max. All the depression falls away from me so fast, as if that stone that was sinking me somehow sunk itself instead. I stand and embrace my friend.

"I thought you were gone!"

Max just shakes his head as if I am being utterly ridiculous. We break the embrace.

"What are you doing out here all alone?"

"Dude, this is quickly becoming the weirdest night of my life," I tell him. "Rack took me out of Sancho's and then was fucking Julio through a bunny suit, so I started walking, and I couldn't find my way out of the alley."

"Shit, that is weird."

I look at Max; maybe it is the way the bright yellow bricks backlight him, but he has an ethereal glow that is both beautiful and unsettling.

"Let's go."

"You know how to get out of here?" I ask.

"Yeah," he says with a sly smile, as if he is the inside man on a hidden camera show.

"Cool."

Oddly, with Max in tow, as if the universe demanded we be together, the golden alleyway becomes just a regular alley. Max and I emerge from the secret passage as if we had license to come and go through whatever dimensions we pleased. I was relieved but also greatly saddened.

Max and I emerged on the street outside Sancho's that had apparently closed in my absence.

Elmwood is a ghost town, especially after the bars close, a lot of times before they close.

"Shit."

"I guess we need to find a place to go," Max says.

I look at my phone, thinking Jenna would have blown it up in full freak-out mode, but fortunately for me, the thing is dead.

"I need to charge my phone."

Max looks at me with concern, and then he searches himself. He finally pulls out his phone. The glass is smashed as if it has been run over by an eighteen-wheeler. "Shit."

"Did you drive here?"

Max's concerned look deepens. He stares at me, as if hoping that I will provide an answer. Finally, he shakes his head.

"Me neither. I guess we can walk?"

Max nods, almost in relief. And we do walk. It feels good to have him next to me. The empty, lonely void that I had been plugging with booze and sex was finally being filled with genuine friendship.

The night is as dark as an oil slick. The stars have all gone into hiding, as if the universe knows to be afraid. The silence is also disturbing; there isn't even a crunch of gravel beneath our feet. Max and I walk in silence for a while; there is a comfort to it, like an old married couple.

"I saw Aria," Max says.

"You did?"

"Yeah, she was leaving town. She seemed upset, Shep."

"She was, or is? We haven't spoken really. I feel bad."

"Do you? I mean really?"

"Yeah, why wouldn't I?"

"Because, Shep, you are a commitment-phobe."

"Fuck you; I have had more girlfriends than you have, Max."

"That's true...for, what, two-month spans?"

I look at him as we share stride for stride. He is right; I am a serial dater. I do seem to find imperfection as soon as the girl du jour gives in and says she really wants the relationship, that she really wants me.

"Yeah, that sounds about right."

"I don't blame you, Shep. These days, why should anyone bother? You know how many blow jobs I've gotten from women with boyfriends?"

"Any of mine?"

Max flashes me a slick smile. "I dunno, Shep; lotta gray area there, and you know how I like the BJs."

"That I do, that I do."

"Besides, you don't date anyone long enough for it to be official, official."

"You wanna clue me in as to who you are avoiding telling me about?"

"Dude! The code!"

Brocode. Never mess with a buddy's girl, even after it's over.

"Sure, like that has ever stopped you."

"Yeah, not with dude's women I didn't know! Shit, Shep, no one would get fucked under those circumstances!" Max protests.

"Right, not a single soul."

"That said, if you green-lit an Aria BJ, I would be OK with it."

"That's generous, Max."

The road seems to be endless; perhaps it is the infinitesimal nature of the dark abyss in which we travel, or perhaps it is something entirely different altogether.

"You never see yourself settling on one woman?" I ask Max.

"It's hard to see me doing any one thing for a prolonged period of time."

I ponder Max's words and wonder if I do not feel the same way. What have I done for any length of time? My job at Insane! Fitness has tenure, but I am always thinking of ways to not stay or to change careers. Maybe Max is on to something.

"But who the fuck knows, Shep? Maybe something will happen; I will meet someone who just slays me so bad that I have no choice. What the fuck do I know?"

"Yeah, what do any of us know?"

"Just that we are gunna die and that we are pretty fucked in the journey to that death, and not in a good way."

"Max, you are getting super dark in your elder years."

"Tell me about it!"

We finally arrive at my house. The lights are on, as if it is some sort of a beacon we have been homing in on all along. Music pulses through the doors as my father emerges in his tighty-whities. He stops suddenly at the sight of Max and me.

"Hey, what are you boys doing here?"

Max and I exchange a look.

"Dad, what are you doing here? Mom won't like it. And what's all the noise?"

"Your mom? Are you kidding me, Luke? You know she is in Florida with what's-his-name."

"Uh...OK. News to me, Dad."

"Are you high?"

I wonder if I am. *What is the effect of rainbow, anyway?*

"No, Dad. Max and I were out; that's all."

"Fine, I don't care, but go to your place. I'm having a thing."

A thing? My place. Maybe I am high.

"Dad, what are you talking about? What thing? Last I checked, I am paying for this house. So..."

"You are fucking high; I knew it! It's OK; so am I. Regardless, you haven't lived here since you finished school. You live with...with...ugh...I forget her name, the Spanishy-looking one."

Max and I exchange looks.

"Dad, what the fuck are you talking about?"

The answer doesn't come, as we are interrupted by two women maybe in their mid to late twenties. One is naked; the other has just panties on. They barely notice Max and me but rather focus squarely on my father, as if he is the most attractive man in the world.

"Daddy..." the naked one coos.

"Way to go, Mr. Shepard!" Max extols.

"Thanks, Maxie."

I stand dumbfounded. This is so odd. Max snaps me out of it smacking me on my shoulder. "We can go to my house."

"Dad, I am coming home tomorrow," I insist.

"Nope! I like my independence too much."

"I *am* coming back," I say to Max.

"Whatever, Shep. Let your dad enjoy his night."

My confusion has me paralyzed. My dad isn't like this; he has made a living pining over my mother in the unrealistic hope that she would take him back. Now he is having a late-life crisis? What the fuck is happening?

Max leads me away from the house, and as if it were never there, Max and I are enveloped in the darkness from which we came. We are on the road but not any road in a town that I have lived in my entire life.

"Where are we going?" I ask.

"You don't know?"

"Should I?"

Max shrugs his shoulders.

"What the fuck was that back there?"

"Your dad?"

"Yeah, my dad."

"It's about time, Shep. Let the old man have his fun; we should all be so lucky at his age or any age."

Max makes a sound point. We walk in silence for a few minutes more, when it becomes clear that there is noise. Feet. Footsteps. Behind us. I stop. Max stops. We stand there and stand facing the abyss. Literally, we are surrounded by darkness. Yet the footsteps are there, like worker ants by the thousands, marching on us, volume blasted to maximum scariness.

"What's the matter?" Max asks.

"You don't hear it?"

"The clowns?"

"What?" I ask.

"The clowns...they always are about this place in the walk, for levity, I think."

"What the fuck are you talking about?"

"Them," Max says, pointing.

And as if on cue, a procession of clowns begins to lumber past us. They wave, grunt, honk their noses, play cymbals, make a funny walk, and some even say hello, as if they have all come directly out of that magical clown car that has miraculous amounts of space. I watch in disbelief, as I realize I haven't a clue what is going on now or perhaps ever. The clowns may be symbolic of levity, but I feel nothing but a growing anxiety.

Max and I watch with differing levels of enthusiasm. I have none, whereas Max seems to have reverted to a childhood place where clowns represent a happy place. To me, it feels as if something is beyond off. The coaster has seeming left the safety of its rails, and no one knows where the fuck it goes, least of all me.

"This shit creeps me out. Can we get out of here, please?"

"Geez, Shep, you sure have a flair for the dramatic. I thought you would appreciate seeing me."

"It's not you, Max; it's them," I say, pointing into nothingness. The clowns have dissipated into the darkness, as if they were nothing but part of my imagination.

"I dunno, Shep; you are acting strange. Maybe we should part ways."

I am suddenly swept up by a sadness so strong that I can barely stand. I don't want Max to leave me alone, yet somehow I am surrounded by loneliness. I stare at the empty space where Max just stood. *Where did you go, my friend? Were you ever really there at all?*

All I know for certain is that I am alone, on this dark unforgiving path, longing for someone to save me from the abyss.

TWENTY-TWO

I don't know where to go, because I don't know where I am. I exist all alone on a black hole of a road that has no beginning or end, only blackness, loneliness, and epic sadness.

I crumple to the ground. The emptiness and abandonment I feel could fill the universe. I wish it would end. I wish for it to be painless. I wish for death.

"What are you doing down there?"

I look up and see Aria. She is a sight for desperately sore eyes. I get up and throw my needy arms around her. Never in my life has human connectivity felt this good.

"It's OK, baby; it's all going to be OK."

Her words soothe me almost instantly, but despite the fact I calm considerably, I don't let go. Aria indulges me and strokes my hair while I hold on to her as if my life depended on it.

"Can we go somewhere?" I ask almost desperately.

"Sure, I know a spot."

I break my needy death grip on Aria, and we look into each other's eyes. I feel like I may weep from both the joy that I am staring at my person, but also sadness that I wasted time without her. I feel like a fool for having judged her and pushed her away. Maybe Max was right about my level of commitment.

Aria kisses me with pouty lips, enslaving my soul instantly. I belong to her in the moment as she takes my hand, and we walk. The togetherness pulses between our hands as if we were one. This is the storybook love that everyone wants and few get to have. It feels as if

I am being cooked in a pot of deliciousness. It is, without a doubt, the nicest I have felt in a long while.

"I want to apologize, Shep."

I tighten my grip on her hand and look at her as we walk stride for stride in perfect unison.

"That night, at the bar, the coke."

I nod.

"I really don't know what I was doing. I told myself it was just to stay up, just to be social. It takes a lot of energy to play this role that people expect, when all I really want is a life with you."

We stop and turn toward each other.

"It hasn't been that long, Aria; how could you possibly think that?"

Aria looks up at me. She seems so tiny and vulnerable in the moment. "When you know, you just know, Shep."

"Why didn't you say anything?"

"Really? Could I have? I wanted to make sure you were good with it."

"Aria, why wouldn't I be?"

"Jesus, do you really not know?"

I look at her, asking with my eyes.

"Shep, you aren't exactly known for keeping anyone around for too long."

And there it is again, as if the darkness that envelops the road in which I walk is my own blackness that I have, yet don't acknowledge. My traveling companions seem to be all too well aware, as if they are acting as my conscience, as if I desperately need them to help me figure it out.

"It's not like that," I protest.

"What is it like?"

I have no answer. Max and Aria may indeed be correct in their assessment of me. They are in a unique position to do so, being that, aside from my family, they are easily the closest souls to me.

"Sometimes it just seems like you are trapped in an existential crisis."

"How do you mean?"

"I dunno, Shep; you are always contemplating a different career, a new place to live. You just don't seem so stable; you don't appear able to commit."

Is she right? Is Max? I never saw it like this.

"I was just thinking, maybe, if you were ready to settle down, you would consider me."

Aria squeezes my hand, cueing me to stop; she touches my face with her other hand, drawing me close to her, and we kiss. It is one of those beautiful, epic kisses, where both participants are fully invested, utterly synchronized, as if in that moment two people connected at the lips have momentarily become one. I am suddenly filled with love, much like the effect of a drug being injected into the system. I am high as can be unionized with Aria.

"I know we aren't ready for a family."

"That would be a big step," I respond. "Then again, is anyone ever ready?"

"Probably not."

"Aria, I am not against the idea. I doubt we can really be fully prepared as to what it might take to raise kids, but it feels way less feasible when there is so much uncertainty at the foundation of us as individuals or as a couple. Shouldn't we be on solid ground before we take on that responsibly?"

"You are making a lot of sense right now, Shep."

"That's reassuring."

"It shouldn't be; I am still debating your commitment issues."

I laugh. She laughs, and we walk in silence through whatever dark void we have been consumed by.

TWENTY-THREE

I wake up in an unfamiliar bed, in an unfamiliar flat. I sit up and drink in my surroundings. The place seems inerently male. There are free weights and an adjustable bench in the corner. Macho movie posters adorn the walls; *Rambo, Predator,* and *Rocky* are the three that I recognize, but there also seem to be Spanish movie posters. They evoke a similar machismo as the American posters, although the films are unfamiliar. The sounds of a shower stop. I hope for a woman to emerge, but I get the opposite. Rack, fully nude, comes sauntering out, cock flopping about like a thick vine in the wind. I stare. I don't want to really, but it is quite a penis, and I find that I cannot look away. He notices me noticing him.

"Shep! You are up," Rack observes, coming to the bed and sitting down.

"Yeah," I say, filled with discomfort as I realize that I too am naked, albeit under a sheet.

"We were afraid we lost you."

"We?"

"Me and Julio."

That's when it hits me. I am in their love nest. I nod as if I am somehow in the know. I am not. I feel that I know the least of what is humanly possible. Rack has a girlfriend, Julio a wife, and I think I have met one of his two kids. Apparently, they are each other's secret gay family, and if I had to guess correctly, I am now part of it too.

"Oh, that's great," I say.

Julio, also nude, comes out of the bathroom next. Now, I am staring at his giant cock.

"Oh, you are conscious. I was worried you had too much rainbow," Julio says matter-of-factly.

"Is there really too much rainbow?" Rack postulates.

Julio shrugs as he sits. Three of us are naked on the same bed, the only thing covering me is a noticeably soft sheet. In an unfortunate series of events, the softness of the sheet arouses me, fully.

"Oh! Not bad for a white boy!" Julio declares. "I told you!" he tells Rack, slapping him on the shoulder.

"Guys, I think you are getting the wrong idea."

"We are?" Rack asks.

"I doubt it," Julio injects.

"I'm not—"

"It's the rainbow, Shep; not to worry. Get in the shower and take care of it; it will go down," Rack instructs.

"Maybe," Julio says, less optimistic.

The thought of walking past these guys with a full-on erection makes me uncomfortable, maybe a bit less than the idea of stroking myself limp in their shower, where God knows what they were doing.

"What the fuck did you give me, Rack?" I ask, annoyed.

Julio pulls off the sheet like a magician's big reveal moment. They stare at my turgidity.

"For one, a hell of a boner!" Julio declares with glee.

I am flooded with embarrassment, and I get up and close the door to the bathroom. I breathe a small sigh of relief. It doesn't last long. I see myself in the mirror, and I apparently have been wearing a mask that I was unaware of. It is a lion.

I am staring at my lion-masked, fully erect self in the mirror. It is odd to be sure. I feel claustrophobic in the mask. I pull on it unsuccessfully, turning like a dog that has been given a cone collar so as not to irritate his wounds. I cannot see the way out of the constriction. Finally, I give up, out of futility, or desperation to lose the rainbow-assisted erection. I start the shower, and after having one last look at myself in the mask, I get in. The shower feels amazing. The short droplets fall on my skin like a welcome home after a decade away. I put my head under the shower head, despite the fact I know I won't feel anything, but I am wrong. I feel everything. I feel what the lion feels as he struts across the plain through a rainstorm. I see what he sees, the possible prey as they rush through the same storm, hoping to make it to home, wherever that may be. I do not chase these creatures; I feel as one with them. I am both the predator and the prey, but mostly I feel as they do, an inherent desire to go home.

The vision ends, and I am far from anywhere that gives me the comfort of home. The shower has become tepid, and I exit, sans stiffness. When I wipe the steam from the mirror, I see the mask is gone, and all that is left is the truth: the rawness of what has been underneath all along—a sad, lonely human just trying to fill his emptiness, just trying to find his meaning, his purpose.

I stare at my reflection as if that will solve that dilemma. I am disrupted by Julio knocking on the door, asking if I am going to come out ever.

"Gimmie a minute."

I have no clothes to put on, but I no longer care. I exit to what appears to be a party. When I exit the bathroom, buck naked, everyone turns to me and looks. The music stops playing, and the silence begins to crush me.

"Oh, it's one of those parties," someone says, stripping down. Soon the rest of the guests follow suit.

The nudity of the room really doesn't make me feel more comfortable, but somehow I don't believe the crowd joining me in my nakedness was intended for my comfort.

People dance, imbibe, nibble on small plates of food as if they are all fully dressed. I have initiated a nudist get-together, quite unintentionally, yet here I am. I do not want to be where I am. I desperately want to leave, but I see no exit to the flat, and I have no clothes to wear in order to leave it. Then it hits me: I know none of these guests. Rack and Julio have disappeared, and I am among nothing but nude strangers. I think to myself that I could take an amalgam of male clothing that must be shed somewhere, yet I see not as much as a thread.

Finally, I opt for the bed, from where I originated. I crawl in and cover myself with the soft erection-making sheet and try to drown out the cacophony of the crowd. Eventually, I succeed, falling into a slumber so sweet, I hope that I may never rise.

TWENTY-FOUR

I am walking down the dark path again, solo, but at least I am clothed. I walk the road, if it even is one, without purpose, almost as if in a sensory deprivation tank; I am alone with my thoughts and my horrible imaginings.

It is such a lonely place, this road, and this life. We walk all alone for most of it until it ends, perhaps on occasion lucky enough to experience some companionship along the way: a lover, a friend, someone who reminds us that life can be a decent place, someone who cares, but, inevitably, that same person who somehow made us whole abandons us in some form or another, returning us to our wilted and fragmented form from which we originated, back where we belong, alone, walking down nothing but a dark and empty path.

"You seem sad, Luke."

I am walking with my mother. She looks somehow younger than I last remember her; perhaps it is an ethereal glow, or maybe it is something else entirely.

"I do?"

"Is it Max?"

"What do you mean, Mom?"

"You don't know? Shit, Luke, I hate to be the one to tell you."

We stop amid the blackness. I look at my mother, but she doesn't have to say it. My heart has sunken already. I feel the road has become empty, I have lost my friend for good, and I know it to be sure. I nod, and she says nothing further.

Like a twin sense, I feel that part of me is gone forever, never to be recovered.

I want to cry somehow, but it is as if the tears refuse to believe the truth and will not acknowledge Max's passing. Instead, I bow my head and think on what my future is missing but also what the past has been. I feel like the weight of my skull may force my chin to crash through my chest.

I imagine the funeral in my mind's eye, although I am the only attendee. I am wearing a dark suit, standing over a shiny mahogany closed casket as it lowers itself into the earth. The day is overcast, as if the heavens themselves are sad.

The casket disappears into the ground, and the hole almost mocks me. It would be easier if it were me in the casket. *No one would miss me. What have I done here with my time? I have made zero significant contributions to society; I am the nothingness of the hole.*

My mind's-eye imagery segues from the dark hole in the ground to the dark hole in the universe, where I seem to exist. The weight from my head lightens, and I lift it only to discover that my mother is gone. I am alone again.

I crumple to the ground under the weight of my loneliness. I close my eyes and not so secretly wish for a quiet and painless end. I wish to be enveloped in the blackness once and for all, rather than to keep unsuccessfully negotiating this dark road I have been on.

I float into a sleep, and for a moment I believe my wishes to end have been answered, but then I wake up in bed again, this time one I recognize. I am at Jenna's.

TWENTY-FIVE

Despite the fact I am in familiar territory, something feels off. I am alone in Jenna's place, something I never have been before. I can't determine if it is that or something else that has me feeling off kilter.

I get up and move to the bathroom. I desperately need a shower, as if the dark road traveled as left me dirty with the filth of the cosmos. I get inside and realize that this may be Jenna's, but the bathroom is somehow *ours*. My stuff is there: shaving razor, toothbrush, comb, aftershave. I am grateful but weirded out too. *Why is my stuff here?*

I take my time, shaving, showering, drying off with my own towel. I didn't realize it before, but I felt spiritually unclean. Covered in cosmic soot, desperate for a cleanse. Now I feel fresh, ready to take on whatever was to be thrown my way. I leave the bathroom towel wrapped around me.

"Jesus, Shep."

I stop short, looking at Jenna, one of her friends I know by sight but not by name, and Bennie.

"Where the fuck did you go? I've been worried sick," Jenna says.

I don't know how to answer. I am stymied by the fact that it seems clear that I share the apartment with Jenna but also by Bennie's presence.

"Yeah, she was worried, like, a lot," Jenna's nameless ding-dong of a friend chimes in.

"Maddy!" Jenna says, as if embarrassed.

"Well, you were!"

I hear the two women prattling on, but I cannot take my eyes off Ben. He returns my gaze.

"You were worried too?" I ask him point blank.

"I was not. I'm just here because I want to fuck Maddy," he says matter-of-factly.

Maddy—who, if you ask me, would be better off unfucked as well as unnamed—slaps Bennie on the chest playfully. Then I realize it. She is one of the women Ben was watching sleep on his phone. I nod in acknowledgment.

"Good to know."

"Dude, I knew you would turn up. Everyone is a bit wigged out with Max and all. No one could blame you."

I nod as sadness sweeps through my soul. All I can think is, *I need to forgive Ben.*

"We good?" I ask him.

"Sure, man."

"You wanna hug it out?"

"Yeah, but only if you put some clothes on. I don't want to turn into Rack and Julio."

"Right!"

"Like, Jenna, your boyfriend has a really nice body."

"Fuck, Maddy, stop checking him out."

"Like, we should have a three-way."

"No, no, no. We are leaving," Ben says, taking her hand.

"We are?"

"Yes."

Maddy seems a touch disappointed but capitulates.

"We'll talk later, yeah?" Ben asks.

"Yeah," I respond.

Bennie takes Maddy by the hand and leads her to the door. She has a pathetic glance over her shoulder at me, pleading with her eyes as if to ask to save her, but all I can think is, *I cannot save myself.*

The door is barely shut when Jenna crosses her arms and scowls. "You want to tell me what the fuck happened back there?"

I wonder if I know how to answer. My life, my reality has been invariably altered, to the point that I seem to be living with Jenna despite the fact I have my own house or used to.

"I'm a bit hazy on a lot of things. I may have accidentally taken some drugs."

"Accidentally? Uh-huh, sure. Did you mistakenly fuck your ex too?"

I look at her, wondering if she somehow knows about Aria; the glance gives me away.

"You did, didn't you?"

"No, I saw her, though, on the road, after Max and I were at my house."

"What the fuck are you babbling about, Shep? Max is dead. You have no house. What road?"

"I know Max is dead. My mother told me."

"Your mother told you?" she repeats incredulously.

"Yeah, I mean, not in so many words, really, but she got the point across."

"What the fuck is happening, Shep?" Jenna sounds alarmed.

I look at her for an answer as to why she is reacting like this. None comes. "What do you mean?"

"You couldn't have spoken to your mom."

"I don't understand."

"Shep, you are scaring me."

Jenna paces a bit. Watching her increases my anxiety.

"Why? Why couldn't I have spoken to her?"

Jenna stops, looks at me, comes close, and puts her hand on my arm, touching me gently. "Your mother is dead. She has been gone for six or seven years. Shep, she killed herself after a long, losing battle with depression."

"That can't be..." I say as my soul sinks.

"Well, it is. There is a history of mental health issues in your family. That is what scares me most, Shep I'm worried you are suffering from this too."

My knees buckle at the weight of this news. It seemed so real seeing her on the road. Jenna catches me, helping me stabilize, and then helps me to the bed.

"I saw her; I swear I saw her."

"Maybe it's the new medication."

"What medication?"

Jenna points to the end table. There is a cornucopia of pill bottles that are so abundant, it is likely that filling them boosts pharmaceutical sales substantially to the point I may well be keeping the entire industry afloat single-handedly.

I get up and look at the bottles, hoping to see the labels that they aren't mine, but they are.

"I need all these?"

"Shep, I don't know. When we started dating, you were already on most of this stuff."

"How long have we been..." I ask, unable to hide my embarrassment at not knowing.

"About two years, living together for the last seven months or so." She pauses. "You don't remember?"

I shake my head. "It's like I've been imagining a different life. One where my mother was alive, and I owned a home. None of that seems true."

"Why don't you lie down, relax, maybe get your bearings?"

I nod. I remove my towel and crawl into bed. It feels like home, although I am not sure why; perhaps it is the depressive in me that longs for the nothingness that only not moving in bed can truly provide.

I am wrapped in the safety of the warm duvet, with only my head peeking out to watch Jenna as she undresses. As little as I can remember, Jenna's body is in much better shape.

She is leaner, with definition lines all over her arms, legs, shoulders, and torso. Jenna is diced. She catches me looking at her.

"What?"

"You look amazing. Are you working out with a trainer behind my back?"

Jenna stares at me, disbelief washing over her face. "Shep, I am wondering if we should take you to the hospital."

"I'm not that depressed. I'm happy to be here and in this warm bed."

"No, not that, although good to know."

"What, then?"

"Shep, I am a personal trainer; we work at the same gym. You manage the place. Ring a bell?"

I swallow as I am afraid to confirm that I do not recognize the life I am in.

"Fuck, Shep, not good."

Jenna is fully nude in front of me. She looks good. Real good.

"Maybe it will come back if I rest a bit. Why don't you come here?" I suggest, lifting up the covers.

Jenna smiles. She moves to me seductively and joins me in the bed. We kiss, a connectivity to be sure, better than the life that apparently wasn't mine somehow; perhaps this is where I have been all along. For some reason, I think of Aria, as if I am kissing her, but it isn't her. *Maybe it never has been?*

"You should just take something," Jenna suggests as she strokes my flaccid penis. "It's your meds."

"Can you get me the something to take?"

Jenna nods and moves swiftly, grabbing a blue tabet and water for me to swallow it with at the bedside. I take the pill. Jenna is beaming.

I wonder how long it will take for the drug to have an effect. My sadness begins to overwhelm me. I feel bad that I cannot perform for Jenna. Clearly, she is invested in me and us, and here I am lost between worlds both real and imagined, and I cannot tell the difference between them.

"I'm sorry," I say.

"It's OK, Shep; I am here for you. We will get through what we need to; I just need you to talk to me, always, and not disappear on me like you did tonight."

I nod. My sadness is replaced by a flush of love; perhaps it is Jenna's sweetness or how much more attractive that makes her, or perhaps it is the chemical aid. Whatever it is, my cock rises, and we are connected in that magical way that couples connect on, both physically, mentally, and cosmically. I don't know how long it lasts, but however long it is, it isn't long enough. I explode inside her for what feels like an hour. Jenna holds me close as I collapse under the density of my epic orgasm, and for some reason, as I fall asleep, I think for a moment of Aria.

TWENTY-SIX

I am in a dream. It's one of those dreams where even though I am conscious of my unconsciousness, it still feels real.

I am on trial. The scene is almost cinematic. Luke Shepard is being judged for his sins, or his life, or, well, something.

I am surrounded by darkness other than a single key light that blasts down upon me as if God is observing from the heavens. I look down and see that I am shackled. My hands are free, but I am in leg chains, and those chains are locked into the ground. I am not going anywhere.

I attempt to block the key light that rains down brightness upon me like an ominous sun. It is a ridiculous thing to do, really. I cannot see anything or anyone.

"Hello?" I call out.

Nothing. A void or more emptiness that I am simply a prisoner of; perhaps I have just been a prisoner all along. There is nothing quite as horrible as when you cannot move. One takes the movement for granted when one possesses it, and yet when it is gone, it is a disaster of epic proportions.

And this is where I am, unable to move in a dream that feels altogether too real. It makes me question everything.

I start to cry, as, without a doubt, I have fallen victim to self-pity. *Where has my life gone?*

"Stop being a bitch," a male voice from above instructs.

"Who's there?"

"We are," a second male voice answers.

The voices sound familiar, but in the darkness, my senses are way off base. Then lights come shooting from the ground level I am on, upward toward my judges, who are perched what seems thirty feet in the air.

Rack and Julio are both lit from two separate lights on opposite ends of the cavernous room I seem to be in.

"Can I please be unchained?"

"I don't think so," Rack says.

"And you aren't even asking properly. 'May I' would be correct. At least you stopped crying," Julio adds.

He's right, I have. "Why am I chained?"

"Ugh. Questions, questions, questions!" Julio laments.

"I told you; he's acting like a bitch," Rack adds.

I have no idea what to do. I am getting upset. "You are calling me a bitch, Rack? Really? Haven't you two been fucking each other senseless behind your girlfriend's and wife's backs?"

They exchange a look, seemingly thrilled with each other.

"I told you," Julio says.

"Yes, you did. Shep, Julio and I think you may be like us."

"How so?" I ask.

"Well, you know, you appear one way and truthfully are another."

"You think I may be gay?"

"We did make out a bit in the alley," Rack points out. "I didn't see you stopping me."

"You took me by surprise!"

Rack and Julio look at each other and snigger.

"Keep telling yourself that, Shep. It doesn't matter to us who you are; we are perfectly comfortable with our love."

"Um...don't you guys hook up in secret? Your heterosexual partners know about this?"

Rack sighs. Julio shuffles in his seat.

"Guys?" I ask.

"This isn't about us, Shep."

"Sure, Rack, this is about me. Maybe I am a little curious somewhere inside here; I don't know. I don't care. This is the twenty-first century; it's all good either way. So why is it so important to you?"

"Not us," Julio says. "Her."

"Her who?"

Rack and Julio's lights go out, and I am left alone again, bathed only in my own light, unable to move. It seems brighter somehow, as if the light is burning through me.

I long to be free of my chains and desperately shuffle my feet in the empty hope that I might not still be attached. A wave of sadness hits me, like an undertalented fighter in the ring with Mike Tyson in his prime, when he was destroying people. I bow my head in defeat. I begin to cry, again.

"Don't be sad, baby."

The voice is female and one I recognize as Aria's. I look up, and sure enough, my new judge, adorned in black and lit as my previous judges were, is Aria. She smiles down at me, and I manage to stop sniveling.

"Aria, I'm so happy to see you."

"Are you? I'm surprised to hear you say that."

"Why would you say that?"

"Why wouldn't I? You were pretty upset with me, remember? I went and got pregnant on you, the drug use, then running off. Don't worry; I would have been pissed too."

"Aria, I'm confused; I was then too. Please give me a break."

"Maybe you should give me a break, Shep. I am carrying your child. You could act responsibly."

"Me? Are you fucking kidding? Weren't you coked up for fuck knows how long?"

"You are being an asshole right now."

"I'm chained to a floor, Aria, and you are playing the asshole card?"

"That's right, Shep; I am. I basically was living with you, coming home to you, playing wife, and then we have a small hiccup in the birth-control department, and you totally freak out!"

I am incredulous. I feel like I may hyperventilate. "Look, Aria, nothing personal, I liked what we had, but I wasn't looking to start a family. I thought you were on the pill. If I am going to take that plunge, I want to have some long-established stability. And a conversation that we are both ready for it. Dating for a few months and getting pregnant by accident don't translate into 'let's get married and start a family!'"

"Shit, Shep, why don't you tell me how you really feel?"

"What had it been? Three months? I'm sorry; no matter how much you try to make me feel bad about this, it won't change anything. I'm not ready. I can't believe you are either."

Aria glowers at me and then she stands. The black judge's robe drapes down her, almost like a tent. She holds her stare. "Maybe this changes something?"

Aria removes the robe. She is naked underneath and clearly very, very pregnant. If she gave birth right then and there, I would not be surprised. I bow my head.

"No! You don't get to look away, Luke Shepard! See what you have done! I'm having our baby!"

I am wrecked with guilt. I love Aria. I let her into my life with such ease, as if she had always been there. It wasn't that I wasn't interested in having a family with her; that potential was there. It just wasn't planned; I wasn't ready. But now seeing her carrying my child, something twitches inside me. Something that does want a baby with her, something that wants a family. There is a hint of readiness, where before there was none. I look back up at her. Aria is still nude, but now there is a Tony Montana–sized pile of blow in front of her. She suddenly has a sinister smile, and once I make eye contact, she dunks her face into the cocaine and takes a massive hit.

"Say hello to our little friend!" Aria imitates.

"Please, Aria, don't!"

"Oh, now you care, Shep? I wasn't just doing drugs to stay awake at work. I was doing them to suppress my fear that you are a full-fledged commitment-phobe!"

"Seriously? You are going to blame me for...for...for this?"

My guilt has converted to anger. Aria is willfully destroying our imaginary child, and I am fucking seething over it.

"Please stop with the drugs! I hate seeing you like this."

Aria nods. "Then you don't have to."

And with that, she swan-dives off the bench, naked and pregnant. I cringe at the idea of her taking that fall with our child in tow, but the robe she is wearing obscures the light, before it hits the ground, yet somehow, Aria never does. She is just gone, leaving only her robes at my feet as a reminder that she ever existed at all.

"She loves you, Luke."

I look up to see my mother. It is her turn to judge now, although she doesn't sit on the bench alone. There is a guy with her. He doesn't wear robes. He wears a tank top that appears to have bronzer on it seeped off from his orange skin. The tank has some ridiculous gym logo on it, and the guy appears to be bursting with steroid-enhanced muscle.

My mother is tanner than usual as well, but hers appears natural, thankfully. Her companion, clearly part Oompa Loompa, sans green hair, smiles at me and then pays attention to my mom in the most disturbing of ways, licking her face with his snakelike tongue. My mother pushes him off her, almost coquettishly. "Stop, Roland."

Roland? Ugh.

Roland does stop, but he gropes at my mother's breasts over her robe, instead. She laughs like a high-school girl being felt up by the captain of the football team.

"Seriously, Ma?"

My mother comes back to reality and pushes the spray-tan muscle head off her, rising a finger at Roland as she does. He is clearly disappointed.

"Roland, be respectful in front of my son."

"Mom, what are you doing with this jackass?"

"Luke, this isn't about me. This is about you."

"Yeah, I'm getting that. The chains sorta send that message home."

"Luke, no one can be judged running loose."

"Clearly."

Roland looks down at me disdainfully, turns to my mother, and says, "Are you sure he's yours? He don't much look like you."

"You know, I think I will meet you by the pool in a bit. I should do this with Luke alone."

Roland looks significantly deflated, flits me a nasty look, and then disappears.

"Who is that guy?" I ask.

"Roland is my fiancé."

"Ugh."

"Luke, I told you this isn't about me."

"Fine, Ma, let me have it."

"This is a crossroad."

"Yeah, and?"

"You want to end up like me—battling depression, full of regret?"

The sudden admission shocks me. I don't know what to say.

"It doesn't have to be like that for you, Luke, but you aren't doing anything about it, are you?"

I am starting to get a crushing headache. I was unaware that dream migraines were a thing, yet here I am.

"I am still suffering, and watching you suffer and be complacent to the point that you are so at home with that suffering makes it altogether much worse for me, Luke."

"I am sorry you feel like that, Mom."

"Are you? What are you going to do about it?"

Part of me has no idea what she is taking about, the other part is well aware.

"If I knew what I was doing, would I be here? Like this?"

My mother nods. "It doesn't have to be so confusing, Luke. I wish I had guidance like this."

"Fine, Ma, guide away."

She nods. "I can't help you, Luke. You have to help yourself."

"I thought I was."

My mother laughs in a way that borders on cruel.

"Well, Luke, as they say, 'You thought wrong.'"

"OK, well, what are you saying is right? Me being chained to the floor here while you judge and educate me?" I shake my chained leg.

"It's for your own good."

"Feels that way, yeah."

"The sarcasm isn't helping your case, Luke."

"And where do you think I am running off to?"

My mother considers this carefully; it seems I may have made a sound point. She waves her hands at the darkness. I hear footsteps coming from both sides of the room. A nervousness shudders me briefly, as unknown creatures move unseen toward me. Out of the darkness comes familiar faces: Michael and Ezra. I am relieved to see them, especially when they remove my chains.

"There we go, Shep," Michael says.

"Thanks."

"Now you know how my ancestors felt," Ezra adds.

"That's dark, man."

Ezra shrugs.

"Can we criticize him from down here?" Michael asks my mother.

My mother ponders his request. She is taking her part in this more seriously than one would hope, particularly if that one is me. "I guess; do you have much to vent?"

Michael shakes his head. "It's less venting and more 'don't do what I did.'"

My mother dismissively waves at him to continue. I look at Michael, who looks at Ezra, and then they both look at me.

"What the hell are you doing?" they say simultaneously.

The words aren't lost on me, although also not lost is that I can move. I shake my legs out a bit.

"Really, guys? What are you doing that I'm not?"

"Shep, this is the only life I will know; soon I won't be able to train anyone aside from geriatrics," Michael says.

"Soon? Isn't that what you are doing now?"

"Fuck off, Ezra!" Michael says, before turning to me. "It's like one day you just wake up, and twenty, thirty years have gone by. You never intend for it to last."

"Yeah, but we're young still," Ezra responds.

"He's got a point."

"Yes, well, that's the problem; it all goes by so fast. Maybe this is your thing, Shep, maybe, but maybe there is more to life. Maybe there is work or a woman you can really be passionate about."

"In his case, maybe a man," Ezra jokes.

"Yeah, Ez, I'm into black guys."

We both chuckle. Michael isn't amused.

"This isn't funny! Shep, you really want to end up like me? My life is sad, lonely, and empty. I survive in this pathetic, miserable world— barely. The shit crushes my soul, and it's my fault! I wish someone scared me straight!"

"Yo, I am outta here."

Ezra leaves, and I am filled with Michael's desperation. I understand what he feels, as if he has transferred all the pain and suffering to me.

"See, Shep, see?"

I nod and try not to crumble into the darkness. "I am sorry, Michael."

"Don't be. It's my doing. Just take heed, Shep; I am a cautionary tale."

Michael puts a conciliatory hand on my shoulder. He keeps eye contact, to the point it makes me uncomfortable, and I have to look away. Michael must take that as his cue, and I feel his hand slip away. I wait a few moments, before looking back, but Michael is gone.

"So, Luke, now you are free. The question is, what will you do?" my mother asks.

I haven't a clue what she means, professionally? Personally? Both? I am so screwed up in this moment, I have no sense of truth or reality.

"I'd like to get out of here to start."

"Yeah, not so fast; we aren't done with you."

"No?"

My mother shakes her head. "Nope. I am, but there are others who get their say."

My father, in what seems to be the uniform of choice—black robes—appears behind my mother. He starts to massage her shoulders. She turns to him disgusted and says, "Will you please give it up? Not happening! Don't you have a midlife crisis to resume, anyway?"

My father removes his hands as if he had been scalded. She gets up and gives him a heated look before turning back to me. "You still have a chance, Shep; don't be like me, don't be like them, don't be like any of us."

I nod acknowledgment, and she is gone like a vapor of smoke, sucked in to an air-conditioning vent. My father takes her seat.

"Hiya, Shep."

"Dad."

"I can't stay; the girls are waiting for me."

"Fine, Dad. I'd like to leave myself."

"Nope! Can't do that, I'm afraid. Everyone's watching! They are counting on it."

"What are you saying?"

My mother comes into view and smacks my dad across the head. My dad cringes.

"Oh, right; sorry, Shep. Too much information."

"Get out of here," my mother tells him.

He does get up to leave.

"What is he saying, Ma?"

"Never mind, Shep." And she leaves too.

I am left alone, and so I pace a bit with my newfound freedom. The light serves as a ballast as I move about in the unknown darkness. I have no idea what I am doing. Even if there was a way out, I doubt I could ever find it without going insane.

And so I pass the time in the nothingness, moving between the darkness and the light, perhaps trying to find my way in the room or perhaps a much bigger notion. At some point I run into something in the darkness. It's on the ground and somewhat soft. I feel as if I am blind, but my guess is that it is a mattress.

"Who's there?" a female voice asks.

"Huh?"

"Who are you? It's a question, dipshit."

I recognize the voice but can't place it.

"My name is Luke."

"Wait. Luke Shepard?"

"Yeah."

Then a lighter ignites, and I can see a bed and a side table where she places the candle. When she scuttles over to the other side of the bed and lights another candle, I see who it is: Lucy.

"Oh, hi," I say awkwardly.

Lucy is dressed in loose pants, and a cut-off top. I can see her breasts, or the under boob, and they are larger than I remember from our tryst in the car. My eyes drift farther south, and either it's the candlelight playing tricks or Lucy is starting to show. She smiles that I have noticed.

"You like?" she asks, rubbing her belly.

"I didn't know."

"No, of course you couldn't have. Now come down here with me," Lucy says, patting the bed.

I get down on the mattress with trepidation, but after standing with the shackles, it is actually very relaxing. I try to keep my distance in a respectful manner, but Lucy doesn't share the same concept. She pulls me down on to the bed and straddles me.

"Lucy..."

"Shut up, Shep," she says, covering my mouth with hers.

Part of me wants to protest, but the one time we had at it was hot, and now for some odd reason, the whole pregnant sex thing is working for me.

Lucy feels that I am ready, and unzips me, expertly sliding me into her. I think no condom, but we already had unprotected, and she isn't in danger of getting pregnant.

That's when things get weird. Other people show up around the bed. My mom and dad for one, and their respective playmates all watch as Lucy rides me.

Then Jenna and Aria appear. They too are pregnant, more so than Lucy.

"Lucy, let the others have a turn," my mother instructs.

Lucy looks at my mom, hangdog, hoping for a change of heart.

"Go on; you've had yours."   Jenna and Aria look for guidance as to who is next.

"Jenna, your turn."

And with that, Jenna gleefully rides me.

"Way to go," my mother's doofus of a boyfriend encourages.

I am getting anxious. I don't know what this means, any of it. My mother smacks her man. "Don't mind him, Luke; just keep fucking."

I want to speak, yet I find I cannot. What would I say?

"OK, Aria, best for last; you were his favorite."

Aria seems pleased at this idea and waits as Jenna dismounts before climbing on herself. She looks at me longingly, which is wholly unlike the others.

"You know I love you, right, Shep?"

She didn't need to tell me. I did know. I nod.

"Aw, that's romantic," Lucy says.

"I love him too," Jenna chimes in a hint of combativeness.

I look desperately around me. Everyone is there—my parents, their real (or imagined) lovers, the people from work, the women I've been involved with recently. I want answers, and I open my mouth to speak, but in truth I haven't a clue what to say or ask first.

"Aw, look at our boy," my mom says to my dad in a rare moment of unity.

I am paralyzed, mostly mentally, and I can no longer delineate as to what is real or dream or what any of it means.

Aria continues to ride me while the crowd seems to get louder and louder almost as if they are some cheering section for Aria to achieve orgasm. My senses are a mess. I taste acid in my mouth as if I may be sick. I smell toast burning; the chanting is louder and louder and completely inaudible, like a radio turned up too much. And my vision is blurred to the point I can't make much but shapes.

That's when the dream finally ends.

TWENTY-SEVEN

I am back home and in bed, alone. My alarm clock is blaring, sports talk radio. They had been playing some game highlights, cheering and what not.

It was all just a dream. I think. I hope. I sit up. I am in my room, in my house, but something is off. I notice several small Internet cameras pointing at my bed.

"What the fuck?"

I move to one of the cameras. They are wireless. A knock comes at my door.

"Hey, Shep, could you put that down? And maybe come outside?" It's Bennie.

I do put the camera down, and I do go outside. I can do this because I am wearing clothes, more specifically underwear. I usually don't sleep like this, and even if I do, it's boxers at best, but now I am wearing colored briefs that are a bit snug, and they seem to be advertising a website across my junk and backside.

I open the door and see Bennie, iPad in hand. He stares down at it. After a moment he looks up at me.

"What is going on?" I ask.

Ben looks at me as if I have six eyes. "Dude, are you tripping?"

"I am going to take a shower and go to work. Will you get the cameras out of there? What the fuck is that?"

"Vleeping, and take as many showers as you want, but you are at work," Bennie says, shaking his head.

I wonder if I am dreaming again. Ben is shaking his head disapprovingly.

"That crap you take is messing with your head, Shep. There has got to be another way."

"The crap I am..."

"Taking, yeah."

I look at him for answer, but it must play as embarrassment of some sort.

"I'm taking a shower, and then I'm going to the gym."

Ben shrugs. I stand in the hallway of the upstairs where the bedrooms are. All the doors are closed. I make my way to the bathroom.

Inside is a mess. It's as if the whacked-out Brady bunch has been living in the home. There are about six towels strewn about, maybe seven toothbrushes in various states, and there is someone in the shower.

"Dad?"

A drop-dead gorgeous blonde, with her hair tied up, pops her head from behind the curtain.

"Hey, Shep."

"Oh, hi, sorry, I didn't mean to intrude."

"It's OK; I don't mind. You wanna conserve water?" the blonde asks coquettishly, sliding the curtain so that I can see her.

She must be in her midtwenties and a gym rat from the looks of it. My cock grows stiff and fast.

"Sure, yeah, why not?"

And I strip in about a nanosecond and get into the shower with a woman I don't even know. I justify that she knows me, and that is well enough, but then again, we are in my house—at least I think it's mine again.

I look at the blonde. She is short and busty with toned legs. I feel like I may explode just looking at her. I grab the woman and bring her in close.

"Your cock is so hard, Shep," she notes, stroking me.

"Put it in your mouth."

And she does, not so expertly, not that it matters. I am done in about twenty seconds, and as soon as I am, I feel horrible. The woman, whose name I do not even know, drinks me down and then stands washing her face of any runaway spunk.

"Wow, you really needed that."

I nod, head hung low, not able to face her.

"You OK?"

"Listen, I'm sorry. I know this is super selfish of me, but you think you could give me a few minutes to myself, if you are done showering?"

I must look ultra-pathetic. She nods. "It's cool, Shep. I gotta get vleeping, anyway. Maybe another time we can pick up where we left off."

"Thank you."

"Sarah. My name is Sarah."

"Thank you, Sarah."

Christ, she knew I had no clue what her name was? I watch as she exits gracefully. I hear as she closes the door behind her. I let the water hit my head. I have a massive headache, and all I can think of is Aria. I am pining. Hard. *Fuck.*

TWENTY-EIGHT

I go back to my room and move all the remote cameras into a closet and put on my gym gear. Before I can get out, a knock on my door sounds. I turn and see Max. I stare at him with utter confusion.

"Dude, Bennie sent me up. Everything OK?"

"Yeah, sure, why wouldn't it be?"

"The cameras? Touching the merch?"

Maybe I am dazed at seeing Max alive and uninjured; it is clear that I am in full malfunction mode.

"Dude, the cameras were bugging me out. What merch did I touch?"

"OK, Shep, you are definitely not OK. We have a business to run. We all are on camera for the vleepers. Ownership isn't immune. Sarah is the merch, and so are you. If we all are fucking each other, we become a porn site, not vleep. For fuck's sake!"

I sit on my bed. My head is pounding. I am not sure if it's from the judgment dream, or is it the rainbow? What is real? What have I imagined? What is happening to my life?

"Shit, Shep, this is worse than I thought."

"I don't think I can go to work like this," I say, looking at Max.

"Dude, you *are* at work."

"At Insane!"

"Huh?"

"The gym, the gym I work at? Insane! Fitness?"

Max shakes his head. "Shep, I have never heard of Insane! Fitness. And I have never known you to work at a gym."

"What? No, that can't be right. I've worked there for almost six years...since I was twenty-three."

"Shep, that isn't possible."

"Yes, of course it is..."

"No, Shep, it isn't! We are both twenty-four. We just celebrated your birthday last month."

I rub my head. My brain just broke into a million little shattered pieces. I get up and move past Max.

"Hey! Where are you going?"

"I need to see for myself."

"See what?"

"Where I thought I worked."

"You can't drive like this. You may be having an aneurysm. I will drive you. Just tell me where."

I nod.

TWENTY-NINE

I direct Max to the gym; all the while he insists that there is no gym where I am asking him to go. And when we get there, I see that he is correct.

The building is there, but it is an abandoned movie theater. I get out of Max's car and stare at the building, as if willing it to change. It does not.

"See, Shep, I told you."

"What about Aria?"

"Who?"

"I was living with her."

"Dude, we are living with a bunch of people, none of whom we can be involved with, other than as work buds."

"Yeah, you said."

"Well, you did sorta break that rule."

"So, it's my house? And our business?"

"Our house, Shep; the business paid for the mortgage off a few months back. You do have your own place, but they only people that live with you are people who work for you."

"You have no idea who Aria is?"

"I do not."

"I need some space, Max."

"Shep, I really don't think I should leave you alone; you are acting like you stepped out of a different dimension or something."

"That sounds about right."

"You hungry? The diner?"

I nod, and we get back into the car. I look at the movie theater, and somehow, I have a memory of something that clearly does not exist. *What is my malfunction? What is life? Is it some existence that lives in multiple universes? Slight differences?*

"I am going to take us to that place where the waitresses are hot. That will make you feel better."

"Yeah, thanks, Max; that sounds good."

"I can't believe you hooked up with Sarah. Dude, she has the most views on our site by far. She's the vleeping star."

"Max, how did you know that we hooked up?"

"Bennie. He has the whole house wired, fucking obsessed with it. Bathroom is off-limits, but he got you and Sarah coming and going."

"Oh."

"I think he's right. We make our money giving people a show; it would be unethical to bang the help, but you get a pass."

"Gee, thanks."

"Thank Ben. Or yourself. You are the top male performer. That's why you get the big bucks."

"I make a lot of money?"

"Fuck yeah, you do. You wanna see your house?"

"Not where we just came from?

"Nope! That's a house and where we do business. Food first. Then I will remind you of what a sick entrepreneur you are!"

I nod. I should feel happiness, but what I feel is numb, and uncertain. I realize I have no idea who I really am. My character has been overprocessed to a degree that I am unrecognizable to myself. What has become of my oneness? Did I ever have any at all? What is real? Or imagined? Who am I? Or who are we?

Are we just the culmination of the present reality—no matter how much that differs from what we think or believe are our truths?

Max pulls up to the diner. It is the standard shit-hole-looking type of place that will have a menu of virtually anything and everything. I am grateful because whatever journey I have been on for however long I have been on it, I don't remember eating on it. I am rapacious.

THIRTY

We pull up to the diner. There is a huge sign outside with the name of the place: Burgatory. I stare at the sign and then at Max. "You're kidding, right?"

"What?"

"Burgatory?"

"Trust me, Shep; you won't be disappointed. Best burger this side of Sodom."

"Sodom?"

"It's a joke, dude. Shit, that crap you have been doing is really fucking you up. You used to have some humor."

"Sorry."

I don't remember having humor. I don't remember having anything at all.

"Don't sweat it. Let's get some food. You will like this place."

I nod, and we get out of the car. I don't remember when I ate last or even if it was real when I did.

The diner on the outside looks like the prototype. It's a long silver-looking tube that could easily be seen attached to a locomotive. From the outside it looks like no one is in the restaurant, but when we go in, the joint is pregnant with patrons. In fact, as we sit, and I have a chance to absorb the room, all the patrons are pregnant, even the men.

Fire in the kitchen flares as if it is ablaze, but it just belches fury on occasion, as if it is reminding us that it is there.

Outside the kitchen appears to be a group of people huddled in prayer. All the people in the circle have their heads bowed, as if some magnificent answer to whatever questions they are asking is about to be revealed.

"This place is tripped out, Max."

"You should take the tour," she says.

I look to see Aria; apparently she is a waitress at Burgatory and, like everyone else, is very pregnant. I stare at her bump.

"It's not real, Shep. Don't worry. Nothing is real. Life is such bullshit."

"You aren't pregnant?" I confirm.

"No, no one is; it's just a sick game."

"That is sick," I agree. "Why would anyone do that?"

"Attention? Isn't that what it's all about now? Don't you guys make your livelihood based on it?"

"Damn right we do," Max concurs.

Aria hands me a menu; it appears endless. She hands Max one too, but he puts his hand up.

"No need, I will have the special."

"Yeah, me too," I capitulate. "Thanks, Aria."

"You know my name? Wow, a bigwig like you? I'm honored."

Aria pulls out her baby, which is a small pillow, and hands it to me. She winks and then walks off to put in our order.

"I think she likes you," Max notes.

"We like each other, a lot more, in a different life, that's who I was asking about."

The pillow is squishy and soft in my hands. For some reason, I draw comfort from it. I place it on my lap for fear of losing it. I have lost everything else; I cannot afford more loss. It could break me to the point where I can never be properly reassembled.

"Guys, I just want to say thank you; my wife and I love your site. So enjoyable!" a random man says, stopping at our table.

"Glad you like it, bud," Max responds.

"You like pillows, Shep? Take mine; I don't even know why I have it." He removes his baby and hands me the pillow. "Such an honor."

Max nods, and the man begs off.

"I feel like I don't belong here, Max. Like my existence is a big mistake or something. As if the universe has passed judgment against me."

"The universe passes judgment against all of us at some point, Shep."

"That doesn't make me feel better."

Max shrugs.

I watch Aria as she hustles about the diner. I ache for her; she felt right on the level of my existence I knew was true. Wherever I am now doesn't feel like existence; it somehow feels nonexistent, as if I have somehow gotten off the beaten path, and I am very lost, with absolutely no hint as to where I have truly been or where I am really going.

"I'm so hungry I could eat my arm off," I say.

"You may have to—look."

Max points his finger around the room. Despite the constant bustle, no one is eating; in fact, customers seem to crane their necks every time a waitress passes by in the hope that they will finally be served. They won't be; no one will.

"Maybe the name is more than a play on words," I suggest.

I look around at the faces bereft of life in some way, and I become exhausted. I take the pillow and bring it to my head; it is beyond comforting. I decide that I need to rest, finally. I use the pillow and lay it on the seat of the booth. I rest my weary head on it.

"About time," I hear Max say.

My eyes grow heavy, but as they do, I see that the patrons and staff are all filming me. The crowd grows around me, everyone looking down at me through the lens of their phones.

I find myself sitting in a dark room, like a movie theater of which I am the only patron. There is a screen, and I watch. The images are of me resting, my head on the pillow; I look content, satisfied somehow, and then I realize that I am no longer in Burgatory but that I am watching my own funeral.

I lay in a casket, and despite that I am watching it somehow, I realize that I am no more.

THE ELSMSFORD HERALD

Luke Shepard, forty-eight, a lifelong resident of Elmsford, Connecticut, was found dead in his home by Aria Winter, his housekeeper. The medical examiner determined Shepard suffocated from gas poisoning. No foul play is suspected.

Shepard is survived by no one. He died alone and unloved, except maybe from the scores of people who followed his "vleep models" online.

The vleeping business made Shepard a very wealthy man. He created the business with two of his childhood friends, who left Elmsford following the sale of their business almost twenty years ago.

There are no scheduled services. Luke Shepard will merely be forgotten as soon as you have concluded reading this.

www.ingramcontent.com/pod-product-compliance
Lightning Source LLC
Chambersburg PA
CBHW070557130626
46556CB00001B/192